Her
VIGILANTE

LILLIAN LARK

Her Vigilante

Copyright © 2020 by Lillian Lark. All rights reserved.
No part of this book may be reproduced in any form or by any electronic or mechanical means, including information storage and retrieval systems, without written permission from the author, except for the use of brief quotations in a book review.
This is a work of fiction. Names, characters, businesses, places, events, locales, and incidents are either the products of the author's imagination or used in a fictitious manner. Any resemblance to actual persons, living or dead, or actual events is purely coincidental.

Editor: Ellie, My Brother's Editor
Proofreader: Rosa Sharon, My Brother's Editor

Content Warning

***

Dear Reader,
Her Vigilante is a taboo romance that is not meant to convey real-life situations.
This is not a police procedural. It deals with violence, death, and unprotected sex.
For an expansive list of content warnings (including those that would be considered spoilers) go to lillianlark.com/content-warnings.
Be kind to yourselves,
L. Lark

***

*To my amazing husband, the Smut Coven,
and the Relief Society.
This wouldn't have happened without you.*

*Especially to Kelsy.
In the best of ways, this is your fault.*

Part 1: The Sin

CHAPTER 1

Evelyn

"Tell me it isn't you." I don't want to play mouse to his cat.

It's quiet on the other side of the phone, a heavy silence. As if the Vigilante can read in between the lines of my words, hear the strums of urgency.

"Give me something, Agent Michaels, and I'll give you what you want. Why don't you think this crime is one of mine?"

Everything about this situation is crazy. This man is my enemy. The person responsible for bloody crime scenes, countless sleepless nights, and scathing emails from my boss. I shouldn't say anything to the enemy, but I need this to make sense.

"The victims are two police officers. Exemplary careers, icons of community police work." I swallow, my throat dry.

This is the moment, the precipice. If he did this, everything I thought I'd known about the Vigilante is wrong. It would be painful. Nine months submerged in the details of the Vigilante murders, only to find that I know nothing at all about the man I hunt.

As the silence grows on the line, I focus on the sounds around me. My hope falls as dread rises.

FIVE MINUTES PRIOR

The scene would have been quiet this morning, before the discovery was made. Peaceful. If an observer depended on sound alone, they could have thought they were anywhere else other than this dingy corner of old warehouses. The cawing of seagulls, the crashing of waves, and the creak of the hanging bodies swaying in the wind.

I lift my face toward the sun, eyes closed, and try to imagine the scene behind me before law enforcement and forensics had swarmed like ants to catalog and analyze. The air is both a tease and a reminder. The taste of salt from the ocean combating the rotting smell of blood having stagnated on concrete.

What was it like this morning? While the unsub, the unknown subject, had done his work?

The medical examiner had taken away the bodies after every feasible photo had been captured in the hopes to find the holy grail to end all of this. Just one hint to give us a leg up, untangle this mess, and deliver… *justice?* An ending, untangling this mess will deliver an ending.

I need an ending.

The scraping of boots on asphalt brings me back to the reality of the people at work behind me. So many eager officials and technicians. This is already so different from the usual Vigilante scene. How quickly they scurry when the victims aren't classified as "taking out the trash," when the targets hit are closer to home.

CHAPTER 1

The mood of the scene is eerie. All the signs point to this being another Vigilante crime scene. The authorities in this area recognize the attributes on sight. Dangling, gutted body in an unusual area. The loud showmanship should be unmistakable.

Hence my presence here. But it's as if someone added salt instead of sugar to a recipe.

It tastes wrong.

I've been chasing the offender the media lovingly dubbed the "Vigilante" for his last eight crimes. Other than the first crimes, the Vigilante has been consistently striking every four weeks, consistently targeting individuals who have "escaped" conventional justice, and consistently notifying the FBI through burner phones sent directly to my desk.

So many crimes without even a whisper of a solid lead. It's enough to keep me up at night, among other things. Things I don't want to think about.

The Vigilante has gotten under my skin. So deep, that the moment I step onto one of his scenes, I can feel it. Something in the air, or the meticulous methods, caresses my senses. This warehouse crime scene doesn't match up, doesn't feel right.

I should turn around and make a list of all of the tiny details of the scene. Make a sound argument that this is not, in fact, a crime done by the Vigilante.

Is that true? Or do I just want it to be true?

The question of the hour. *Am I objective enough to make that judgment call?* I falter.

There's no reason to think I'm being biased. No one else sees me as being biased about the Vigilante. They just see an FBI agent who is driven to apprehend this perpetrator. They don't know what his phone calls do to me.

A clatter has me turning.

"I-I'm so sorry, sir, special a-agent, sir." The hapless tech looks up at my partner, shaking in his boots. I bite my lip. My behemoth of a partner wears the suit of a fed but has the standing of a soldier and the air of a drill sergeant. People in the office called him *Full Metal Jacket* in whispers. The similarity in the face is uncanny.

Special Agent Jeremiah White stares down at the tech with masked exasperation. "Get back to work." Never mind the fact that he has no authority over the tech, the kid hurries away. Jeremiah approaches me as he shakes his head. "They get younger every day."

"I think it's actually that you get older every day," I muse. "You're going to turn around someday and be surrounded by kindergarteners. Then you'll know it's time to retire."

He glares at me. "I've been told you pressuring me to retire is discrimination and I should report it."

I hum. "But then who would be your partner? They'd pair you with Gables. Can you imagine doing this with Gables? He's so… shiny."

Jeremiah ducks his head, so I don't see him smile, but his height makes the gesture useless. Watching his rockface crack is the most enjoyment I'm going to get until we get through this crime scene. I cling to it.

Gables isn't so bad. Just earnest. I used to be earnest like that.

This bit between us plays like a record. The normal part of our workday that we repeat as a ritual when everything else is a hurricane around us.

Our pairing is an unlikely one. The "perfectionist" with the agent on the edge of retirement. We were matched because we don't get along with anyone else. Jeremiah is like a bull, a gray, weathered bull. He refuses to bow or step around any egos he works with. I suspect that being assigned as my partner is a punishment. The surly bastard had undoubtedly pissed off someone with power, broke the china.

I'm his penance.

We shocked everyone when we clicked.

It wasn't shocking to me. Jeremiah treated me as an asset instead of stumbling over the fact that I'm good at what I do. A breath of fresh air in a world of stagnation.

"Well, the techs look just as scared of you. Maybe your title is intimidating," Jeremiah says.

I snort. "Oh yes. I'm the terrible, heartless Ice Queen. The villain trying to stop the Vigilante from saving those the justice system doesn't…. You'd think the news would come up with something better." It only stings a tiny bit that there's a kernel of truth in the headlines.

"I mean, at least you're newsworthy. They don't even pick on me. I'm invisible." My partner pretends to pout, and we share a chuckle. He sighs, and it's back to business.

Jeremiah rocks on his heels, taking in my vantage point of the crime scene. The dark stains on the concrete and the litter of number cards being used by the techs. The strength of the sun on my blazer is uncomfortable but I keep my position. Considering.

"Two victims instead of one," Jeremiah starts.

"I called the office. No burner phone has been delivered. And this is off schedule."

He nods. "Something is off."

A tension I'd been unaware of leaves my shoulders. It isn't just me who notices. I'm not so far gone I've become delusional. The relief is a beautiful thing.

Jeremiah scratches his ear. "He could be changing his MO. It wouldn't be the first time he's changed the timing. This warehouse isn't far from the first warehouse victim." He pauses, hesitant to mention the real deviating detail. "And the victims… are we sure their reputations are as spotless as they seem?"

I bite my lip. "As sure as we can be."

We pause. I hate unknowns.

"I should let you know that I'm going to do something… unwise," I say. It is only fair that I warn Jeremiah. The disciplinary action I face could affect him.

My reputation has always been about doing the right thing. I've been torn apart in the media for not having a heart or the town I came from, but they've never been able to fault how I do my job. This one moment could ruin everything. The wolves are at my back. Within my own mind and externally.

What do I choose? To shield myself or get the answers to stop this from happening again? Because this will happen again. The bright violence of this will be too much for the unsub to resist repeating.

When the next victim surfaces, will I be confident that I investigated every avenue?

Jeremiah's mouth thins in displeasure. "Should I ask what you're going to do? Or pretend I don't know about it? That I don't see you holding your cell phone like a lifeline. I'm assuming Gloria isn't the one you're debating calling right now." Intensity inflects his voice. "Will it be worth it, Evie?"

Always so damn observant. The slight warmth in my chest battles the fluttering panic and anticipation, it makes my smile wry.

"I shouldn't have told you about Gloria," I stall. Jeremiah gazes down at me, waiting for my response to the rest of his statement. "Ignorance is bliss… I won't know if it's worth it until I try."

He snorts but casually strolls around the busy techs to the other side of the crime scene. Plausible deniability.

As long as I'm open about the call with my higher-ups, the case itself won't be at stake from my actions. There will be an investigation into my state of mind. If that investigation has any depth whatsoever, my time as an agent will be over.

I've been partaking in mind games with a killer for months. I am the definition of compromised.

I pull out my phone and type in the number from memory. The number that had called the last burner the Vigilante sent. Attempts have been made before from our techs, and he's never answered. But an attempt has never been made from *my* phone.

The simple ringtone is dissonant in my ear, jarring and unpleasant. I hold my breath. It rings and rings. I swallow, no one is going to pick up. I disconnect and analyze my phone screen.

I start to catalog my reaction; is it relief or disappointment that makes it feel like something is lodged in my throat? Honestly, I can't say. I squeeze my eyes shut, trying to close the door in my mind that I'd opened. It doesn't matter, I can't have really expected him to pick up. Nothing matters but doing my damn job.

My ringtone sounds and my heart rate spikes when it displays the number I just called. The trill isn't a loud sound in the clammer of the crime scene. No one notices as I accept the call.

The other side of the line is silent. I don't know what to say now that the phantom from my dreams listens. Luckily, he speaks first.

"Special Agent Evelyn Michaels, you called?" he purrs. The words are edged with satisfaction and danger. Why shouldn't he be satisfied? I violated all the rules by calling him first. I've lost this round, flipped the board game. The pieces scatter away too fast to catch, never to be seen again.

"I'm surprised you called back." I'm more surprised with how level my voice sounds. My heart beats overtime.

"I had to cover my tracks first, make sure it wasn't a trap to get my location. If I wasn't such a careful person, the chase would have been over a long time ago and you wouldn't think about me at all."

The blood rushes in my ears. My laugh is a bitter one.

"Because your goal is just to get me to think of you? So, we can stop this whole charade now?" I wince, *Way to go, Evie, confirm you think about him.* Embarrassing, but not the worst. The ultimate truth is that there isn't any part of my day that I don't think about him. "I'm standing in front of a crime scene that looks just like yours."

A musing hum comes from the phone.

"So, you think that it's what? A copycat? That must be so inconvenient for you. To have multiple vigilantes rising, the havoc would be unimaginable."

The words are careless. His enjoyment of this is obvious. What exactly about this is he enjoying? The spread of his ideology or the simple joy of messing with me?

"Tell me it isn't you."

"Give me something, Agent Michaels, and I'll give you what you want. Why don't you think this crime is one of mine?"

CHAPTER 1

"The victims are two police officers. Exemplary careers, icons of community police work."

The silence has gone on too long. He isn't going to answer the question I risked my career to make. How does my sigh sound over the phone? Exasperated? Disappointed? Heartbroken? For the love of God, anything but the last one.

Woodenly, I start moving to end the call. The man's voice slices through the phone line with a growl. It's a sound that's going to make it hard to sleep tonight.

"It wasn't me."

Does the Vigilante sound angry? Relief overwhelms my senses. I can breathe.

"Okay then." I hang up the phone before he can respond.

No need to further spiral. I have things I need to do. I pull up my email and send a request for a copycat expert. There's a new killer to catch.

CHAPTER 2

Evelyn

Someone pushes past me as if I'm moving in slow motion and the coffee in my to-go mug sloshes. I could be moving in slow motion. There is a heaviness to my every action that hadn't been there just last week.

Management acts like they're unhappy I called my bereavement-leave short, but I see past their masks. They're relieved they don't have to reassign the Vigilante case. I had only enough time at the last location to do a press conference before Gloria had called me and told me about Malcom.

I'd flown from there to the small town I'd clawed myself from to attend the funeral. Shades of mourning black and weeping people. I'd done my best to ignore my grandfather, and he'd returned the favor. I held the hand of the woman I considered a mother as they lowered the best man I'd ever known into the ground.

Gloria and Malcom Bates took me in when no one else wanted to incur the wrath of the local preacher. I hadn't visited them since being recruited by the FBI. I always said my workload was too much for me to get away. In reality, I struggled to make myself go back to the town that had ostracized me.

CHAPTER 2

If I let it, the guilt will swallow me whole. The guilt that I didn't brave the whispers and glares to visit the most important people in my life. It's too late to atone for my cowardice. Malcom is gone.

Even still, I tried to stay. Tried to make amends for the fact that it had been years since I'd last visited.

I couldn't. I couldn't listen to people talk. Couldn't pretend that I wanted to be in that terrible town for any reason other than to make sure Gloria had someone to lean on. Sleep evaded me. I'd wander the dark rooms of the little home Gloria and Malcom had shared like a zombie until Gloria had grabbed my hands in hers and squeezed.

"I want you to go. I love you, Malcom loved you, but you aren't going to deal with the grief you feel here. This place is poison to you."

She had been right. So here I am. Back to work. Jeremiah's look is dark with disapproval as I approach our desks.

"You shouldn't be here."

I agree with him in my head but refuse to acknowledge anything. I will not give ground.

A stack of papers with a burner phone in an evidence bag sit on my desk. "What is this?"

"You had a delivery to your desk. I had a hunch, so I took the box to evidence. They're doing tests now, but no one thinks they will lead anywhere. That was the only thing in the box."

I raise my brows. A hunch. I choose not to get annoyed that he opened my mail on a 'hunch' because honestly... I'd do the same. Instead I pick up the evidence bag and turn the burner phone in my hands. The hair on the back of my neck raises. Who would send this?

"I've kept my eye on it. There haven't been any calls yet—"

Jeremiah is interrupted, we both jump as the burner phone comes to life in my hands. For all that it felt like I was moving through molasses a minute ago, I'm quick now. The world comes into focus as I glove my hands, open the bag, and take out the phone.

"Evie—"

I shake my head at Jeremiah as I answer the phone. I'll tread any road required to do this job. Anything is better than the soul-numbing grief that waits for me when my mind wanders.

The sound of an open line crackles over the phone. Maybe breathing. A gravelly voice cuts through the soft static, deep and male. The sound of it has my scalp tingling. A primal instinct identifies him. A predator.

"Special Agent Evelyn Michaels, I saw your press conference. You perform cool under pressure. I admire that in a person."

"Who is this?"

"Don't be coy. You know."

I do know. The Vigilante is on the phone with me. Of all the impossible things.

"I'm just calling to tell you something. A gift, maybe, from me to you. I'll wait for you to get a paper and pen, the red one from your desk should do."

The sense of being watched is overwhelming. Jeremiah had come up right next to me so he could hear the conversation, we share a look. I don't hesitate to grab the red pen on my desk.

"I'm ready."

The man on the phone rattles off an address before hanging up. I look at the burner phone, white noise fills my ears as adrenaline pumps and the grief accosting me returns to being a bad memory.

"We have another crime scene."

***

CHAPTER 2

I cast a glance over the bar patrons again, and I see him. My target for the night.

There's a tug in my chest. A need for something after having dealt with the copycat's crime scene. After hearing the voice of the Vigilante taunt me. The rest of the day had gone as well as expected. Following up on whatever leads we can. Interviewing the deceased officers' families. The whole time a craving had been building in me. I'm tense and restless.

It's a craving I recognize. An old bad habit come back to haunt me, but I need to be able to focus. I'll feed the monster in bites to better devote myself to this case in work hours as I have since being assigned the Vigilante case.

The blonde wig I wear to cover my dark hair itches, but I ignore it while I sip my Coke, hold the rum. No drinking while hunting. I want my senses sharp. I want to feel every moment of the interaction.

The wig is the most I do to hide my identity. Anything more would be superfluous. I barely spend any time with the men I approach. They won't be able to pick me out of a lineup. They won't be able to tell sordid tales to the media.

Why has this habit resurfaced now? These urges that tickle my senses, making it hard to focus. So many possible answers to that question. I've spent some time pondering them. I keep coming back to the sound of the Vigilante's voice. The notes it cracks on, the parts where his voice is smooth and runs over me like the seeping chill of snow.

That voice is a connection. An insidious, impossible connection. Forged from the first moment I answered the trilling phone and heard the growl of the man's voice. I don't know what about his voice had woven through and tugged me on this chase but tug it did. That moment marked the beginning of the downward spiral.

Telling myself that my issues stem from my obsession with the Vigilante lets me avoid the monster of grief that still snaps at my steps even so many months after Malcom's death. Being obsessed with the Vigilante, waking from dreams panting in a pool of confusing emotions, body tight in unrequited tension, is better than dealing with the shadow of death that touched my life.

Before the Vigilante, the cases I worked on had been singular challenges. Challenges that didn't invite obsession. A connect the dots of a morbid sort. I do well when it comes to winning those types of games. Always rushing forward to prove myself. Charging to the bitter end.

The Vigilante case is a bitter long haul in comparison. And it feels… personal. As if the ink from the countless pages I've read has seeped into my soul and taken up residence. A stain visible under the media spotlight.

My target nurses a beer, not giving the rowdy crowds around him any attention. The way he keeps his head down is what triggered my interest. I don't go for the men that take up space and eye their surroundings like they can exert control by their sheer force of will.

I always pick my targets carefully. Try to make my actions as safe as possible while still getting what I need. What I've needed since sneaking into men's cars when I was a teenager. To feel filthy.

Sinner, slut, daughter of Eve.

When I was younger, I chased the sensation of power. Embracing the light feeling I got from being sinful. A contrary "fuck you" to the first man who raised me, spewing hate from his pulpit. It's always interesting that one can feel so powerful while being on one's knees.

Counseling had helped the urges. After I had moved in with the Bates and enrolled in therapy, I could almost pretend I was normal. But when life starts to untangle like the string on a sweater, it becomes clear that those sorts of urges don't disappear. They are merely restrained by cheap yarn.

As an FBI agent, I'm aware that my behavior is dangerous. As a person who has to live in my own head, the danger is worth what I get from this power exchange. To try to combine both mentalities, I have a list of requirements for my targets. No wedding rings, no assholes, and no alpha males.

I make my decision. The best candidate is the nondescript man at the bar.

Jeremiah

I turn the key in the ignition, turning off the engine. I'm parked in front of a local bar. Evie chose well tonight. This establishment is far enough away that she won't run into any off-shift law enforcement we're working with but close enough that she doesn't feel like it's an inconvenience to me.

I ease back in my seat to wait. It won't take long. I don't like to go into bars, the alcohol on the shelves causes an itch between my shoulder blades. A craving that I can't indulge in. My rule is no drinking while on duty. Until I take my partner back to our motel, I'm on duty.

Evie being here is her vice. I had expected her to break soon. My one requirement when she breaks is that I drive her home. It provides me peace of mind to see her get back to safety without some man getting attached to her. Why a guy would think to approach a woman who is sharp enough to cut and licensed to carry is beyond me. But it happens.

Our dynamic is a unique one. We support each other. Watch out for the other. Keep each other's vices from interfering in the case.

We both know our coping methods are unhealthy, but it's better to have someone ready to pull you from the edge than to have no one at all. Before I partnered with Evie, I had no one. It had been my own fault. I had been resistant when we were first partnered. Resistant to be a friend, to let someone else in for me to disappoint, but Evie and I relate on a level I've experienced with few people.

Maybe one day we'll take the time to address the underlying infection instead of merely keeping each other in line.

That's not something that's going to happen with the Vigilante still on the loose.

Light spills into the parking lot as the bar door opens and my wayward partner steps out, a bounce to her step that hadn't been there before. I want to shake my head at it all, but am only going to do the expected amount of pestering about her hobby.

Evie ducks into the passenger seat and shoots me a relaxed smile. I shake my head, not allowing myself to spend any time looking at her mouth. Evie is not a woman that I think of in that way.

"What's it been, three weeks?" I don't have to ask. Both of our compulsions line up with the Vigilante's schedule now. Instead of starting a conversation about the similarity of our behaviors to the killers we investigate, I harp on my regular points. "Have you even gotten test results back from the last time? You wouldn't have to worry about screening if you used a rubber."

Evie purses her lips. "Have you ever sucked a cock through a condom?"

I cough, trying hard not to laugh.

"Let me tell you, it isn't pleasant. The texture is abhorrent."

Evie smiles at my poorly hidden mirth. Do I like this practice of hers? No. Do I badger her about it? Always. Do I judge her for it? Never.

The shit we've seen…. If it eases her mind to suck off strangers, it isn't the worst coping skill I've heard of. Every person who does the work we do has some sort of self-destructive compulsion they keep under wraps. Evie's is just creative.

Evie blows out a breath. "Thank you for picking me up."

"Don't mention it. My pleasure. There is never a better time to tease you about your preferences."

Evie's ringtone goes off. She never changed it from the factory setting. Since everyone changes their ringtone from the factory setting, it still manages to be unique. My fearless partner glances at the phone screen and declines the call.

I suck my teeth. "You should call her back. She just cares about you."

Evie sighs and looks through the windshield. Her face open and heartsick. "It just isn't something I can deal with right now."

"You call her as soon as we wrap up this case. She wants to be in your life." My tone is definite. She has been screening the poor woman's calls for months. Grief is a hard thing, but Evie isn't the only one who is suffering.

"Are you going to call Marcus then if I'm going to do the right thing and call Gloria?"

Pain stabs my chest, and it's hard to breathe. It doesn't matter how many times the topic of my son comes up; it will never not be painful. The pain is a good thing. The day that I'm too numb to feel the loss is the day my life stops being worth living.

"I'm sorry, I shouldn't have said that. It was thoughtless and horrible." Shame is stark on Evie's face.

I clear my throat. "The difference is that Gloria is reaching out to you. Don't keep hurting her with your silence. The woman lost her husband the same time you lost Malcom."

Evie looks down and nods. Good. If I can keep my partner from repeating my mistakes, it will be worth any discomfort.

"She leaves voicemails," Evie says. I'm surprised she wants to talk about something so emotional. She projects a chilly façade, but we understand each other better.

"Voicemails?"

"With little motivational things Malcom always used to say, Malcom-isms."

Evie swallows. We're treading on fragile ground here. "Even if I don't have the capacity to call her back, I listen to those messages over and over again." Evie sighs. "I'm just saying to keep trying, Jeremiah. Marcus could do the same."

My throat swells at the idea. It's a nice thought, no matter how unlikely.

CHAPTER 3

Evelyn

I wake, gasping. Sweat slicks my skin and my body is strung taut. The motel sheets wrap around me tight in a restricting mess. I quake as the last bits of the dream fade.

The deep sounds of the voice are slow to evaporate.

It's a nightmare. Just a nightmare. Only a nightmare.
It wasn't a nightmare.

No matter how many times I define it as a nightmare in my mind, my body knows the truth. Truth and logic craft my world. Denying the truth is its own spiral. One I'm struggling to withdraw from.

I shift my hips; the smallest movement and a moan escapes my lips, recalling the phantom sensations of a man's hands. The rasp of words in my ear. I try to take a breath; to calm my body down. My breath comes out shaky; my lungs needing me to pant. My heartbeat thumps under my skin. It's like trying to stop a train.

My body is on the very edge of ecstasy. It just needs the slightest push. A breath on a feather.

It's wrong. It's sick.

I trail my hand down my stomach and slide it into my underwear. I'm so sensitive. So wet. Temptation and logic war in me. *How else will I get back to sleep?* I turn my face and hold the pillow over it. I bite down.

I spear myself with two fingers with an unforgiving curl in and up. The crush of my hand against myself and my own rough treatment has the freight train screaming forward and I come and come. It's pain, punishment, and salvation. Every pulse destroys me with hot pleasure and muffled cries until I'm empty and wrought.

Finally, I stop muffling myself and breathe in the air chilled by the motel AC. Tears prick my eyes and the comedown from the climax lodges a jagged-edged shame in my chest. I pull my wet fingers from myself.

Why? Why does he affect me this way?

He's just a voice, just a man playing mind games. The dreams are never anything concrete, but my body feels possessed.

I shiver as my sweat cools and pull myself upright. There will be no more sleep tonight. I might as well start working.

***

I take my first hot sip of coffee, hoping to burn away the fog my disturbed sleep has cast over my thoughts with the bitter brew. It almost works. Another cup and I might not be considered a zombie.

"Coffee is life," I proclaim as I fall into the passenger seat of the car Jeremiah rented. The smell of sausage has my mouth watering as Jeremiah hands me a foil-wrapped cylinder.

"Is that what I think it is?" I ask.

"I figured you would appreciate a breakfast burrito to go along with your caffeine." Jeremiah's smile is wry.

"You are the best. This is why I can't let you be partnered with Gables. You're too good for him." I unwrap the delicious offering and bite into it with gusto. The flavor of savory sausage and eggs giving me as much life right now as my coffee. I just barely keep my moan of pleasure to myself. In the light of day, surrounded by normal things, the last bits of my obsessed dream finally begin to vanish.

"Bad night?"

"I've had better." Before being assigned to the Vigilante case. "But I had the opportunity to make a new list of interview questions for those people we were going to interview about the Tomlin case."

I pass the notepad to Jeremiah who scans the questions at a stoplight and nods. "You think we can get better information than what we were given?"

"I think we can get different information. Tomlin is the first known victim. The Vigilante is bound to have messed up somewhere, why not during his first time?"

I sneakily take in Jeremiah's demeanor. His eyes aren't quite bloodshot and he doesn't smell as if he's been imbibing. He isn't too worse for wear. He must have drunk just enough liquor to help him sleep. Not for the first time, I'm tempted to use that coping mechanism. If only to sleep. But I already have my issues. It's better to not add to them.

I've seen what that kind of dependence can do. I keep an eye on Jeremiah's habits so I can intervene before he devolves.

After this case, I'll bug Jeremiah about going back to AA meetings. It hurts that my hesitance to push him stems from my desire to avoid his comments about my own vice. It's selfish, but I've been told I'm selfish before. It's not a new title.

Not like the title I'd get if anyone else in our department found out about my vice.

I suspect my coping mechanism to be the most original out of our colleagues, but I'm not going to tell the department psychologist about it. That man has already diagnosed me with enough things to keep him busy. No need to add the thrill of anonymous oral sex to my folder.

When I told Jeremiah that Dr. Collins said we got along because I have daddy issues, I thought I'd have to perform CPR with how hard he laughed. The diagnosis makes as much sense as anything else in my life does.

At the beginning of our partnership, I had asked Jeremiah why he was the only colleague who didn't grouse about my performance. Who didn't want to go over the ways I could improve even though my methods result in success while theirs don't. Jeremiah is the only colleague who values me.

My partner didn't respond right away. We sat in silence as I waited for his answer. The generic diner coming to life around us. Early morning sounds of clattering silverware and murmuring conversation at other tables had me itching to fill the silence. I had to bite my tongue to keep from inserting a flippant remark. It was important for me to know why. Worth the tickling discomfort.

When Jeremiah met my eyes, it looked as if he had aged a decade.

"Do you remember the Baker case?"

Another space of silence, this one was full of understanding instead. That case had been horrific according to the news. The instructors covered it during my time at Quantico. Mother, Allison Baker, goes missing and everyone suspects the husband. Authorities can't prove anything. The woman's sister goes missing next. Still no leads. FBI called in for a consultation because the father had custody of twin boys, six-year-olds.

One of the boys started talking to a teacher at the time. Saying incriminating things about the father. Authorities were called but arrived too late. Father killed the twin boys and himself.

Some details about that case still haunt me, and I only saw poor quality photographs. The man had used a machete.

When Jeremiah spoke, his voice was full of helpless fury. "If your methods can stop that from happening again. Then I'm with you. I support you. I'll fucking pray to you if prayers made any difference."

I flinched at that. I didn't want anyone praying to or for me.

After that morning in the diner, our partnership had become something more unconventional than what other agents have.

"Have you heard back from the office about sending a copycat expert?"

A rude sound comes out of my mouth as I take another bite of burrito and shake my head. Chewing and swallowing before speaking.

"I got one email that said that my request will be put through the channels and we should proceed as if this is the Vigilante."

Jeremiah sighs. "Should have figured. You didn't want to tell them about the… phone call you made?"

"I typed it up in my report. They obviously didn't read it." I had held my breath after sending that email, but they put off reading any reports from me until the last possible moment.

Jeremiah grunts in dissatisfaction.

CHAPTER 4

Evelyn

We stand over a conference table at the local station. A whole conference room, what a boon. Last time we were at this station for the first warehouse murder, they gave us the equivalent of a broom closet to work in. How the times have changed.

The morning light is bright as it comes through the blinds and glares off the reports and glossy photos. Having everything laid out like this helps mental organization.

The reports covering half of the table are from the first three murders done by the Vigilante. Confirmed by the media and the untraceable info packets of the victim's crimes released after the bodies were discovered. It's assumed the Vigilante is the one that releases that info, but it's not like he signs anything.

The other half of the table is sparser in comparison. Including information and photos from the crime scene of the two victims yesterday.

The differences between the two sides are vast. It isn't bias. It's fact. A truth ringing so loud that even I can still hear it.

The first Vigilante victim was Ralph Tomlin. Found hanging and gutted in the garage of his own suburban home. The man had been tried for the charge of sexual assault of a minor. The girl was his niece. The trial fell apart when the girl recanted her testimony. After his body was found, it became known that the man had recorded the crime, several times.

The second was a drug dealer who bribed officials to look the other way. Found in his car, throat wrapped with rope to the headrest, gutted. This was the most different of the Vigilante crimes because of the presentation of the body. It had originally gone unidentified until an info packet came out. The officials involved in the bribes were fired and charged.

The third was the warehouse case. A man who had been tried for home intrusion and murder of the occupants. Found not guilty because evidence went missing. That was the first case Jeremiah and I had been called in for. This is the one that looks most like the scene we had seen yesterday morning.

A hanging body slit across the middle, deep enough for things to hang out, blood pooled artfully beneath it. This scene setup became the Vigilante's signature.

When I look at the photos on the other side of the table, they appear nothing alike.

Yesterday's crime had two victims. Police officers from a different area who had been on patrol. It's assumed the unsub had gotten them on that patrol and moved the bodies to the warehouse. Arranging the scene to be similar to the Vigilante. The blood spatter evidence suggests that at least one of the victims was still alive when they were strung up.

CHAPTER 4

The Vigilante's victims are always dead before he positions the body. A lethal injection of drugs. It's worth noting because the executions don't appear to be about making his targets suffer. The deaths seem as if they are more a warning for others.

The full-color headshots of the victims from yesterday pull my attention. The young black woman looks proud in her uniform. She doesn't smile, but the happiness is there. Officer Elizabeth Kerry was only a few years out of the academy. Her partner was a veteran officer. The headshot next to hers shows the jovial older white man with a giant salt and pepper mustache. Officer Peter James looked like he could play Santa Claus if he had grown a beard.

The reports we have so far say the unlikely duo were very close.

The media hasn't picked up the story yet. Probably still working on the expected timeline of the Vigilante. It's an opportunity. If we can prove it's a copycat, then we can keep the media from speculating on what crimes that these officers committed. They would assume guilt.

The age difference of the partners is only a little greater than Jeremiah and mine. I clench my jaw. Purpose or opportunity? A message or by chance? The hairs on the back of my neck rise.

"Jeremiah, until this is over, wear a vest."

Jeremiah stops his note-taking and gazes at me silently before continuing making a list of the tasks for this case. That he doesn't argue helps the constriction of my throat ease, and I continue my analysis. A bulletproof vest is going to be so uncomfortable in this heat.

We are point on this until the expert gets here, maybe even after that too. If an expert gets here.

Jeremiah and I are the most informed agents on the Vigilante murders. Experts are good at what they do, but there isn't anything quite like having on-the-case experience.

A knock on the door disturbs us. Lt. Eisenhower stands there stiffly. His dislike for all the business involving feds being in his station is obvious, but neither Jeremiah nor I take it personally. Our boss is an asshole and creates contention everywhere we go before we even get there. It's a gift.

Lt. Eisenhower is a fair person, broom closet withstanding. He's never obstructed our investigation and is always willing to give us manpower when requested. He is in the category of being more courteous than some other authorities we've worked with.

Behind the lieutenant is a rookie-looking cop carrying a box of folders and a man in a suit.

The lieutenant lifts his extremely bushy brows. "Agent Michaels, Agent White, the files you requested. And this man." The lieutenant nods to the suit. "Says he's here at your request too."

Jeremiah is the first to stand, delightedly surprised. "Ah, the copycat expert."

Lt. Eisenhower furrows his brow. "We're sure it's a copycat then?"

Surprise has me straightening, I assumed that the lieutenant would hop on this possibility. It isn't standard to suspect guilt of fellow officers. Then I see it, the relief surfacing from guilt hidden under the man's brows.

Catching the Vigilante has never been law enforcement's priority. The unsub targets the people that law enforcement are helpless to stop, those untouchable

CHAPTER 4

through legal channels. There exists an odd kinship that officers feel toward the Vigilante crimes.

The lieutenant hasn't been open about it, but I suspected that he, like all the other authorities we work with, believes in the work the Vigilante does. As if the Vigilante is an angry god or an angel, smiting the guilty.

This case would cause a conflict of faith. To have faith in a serial killer they've deemed God or in fellow officers with no record of wrongdoing? How deep does their belief in the Vigilante go in order to make them doubt the very people they work with?

What kind of guilt would a cop carry that a criminal they had treated as a deity in the past has changed their MO to strike at innocents? A lot.

Or am I biased because I've seen what blind faith does? I shake my head. Whatever personal reflection the lieutenant has to do is up to him to deal with.

As far as I'm concerned, they're all guilty as hell for taking comfort in the Vigilante's work. They possess authority, not the anonymous criminal picking up where our system fails. The Vigilante's work is what inspired this copycat.

I'm not the best judge though. I'm the guiltiest among us, I've kept my personal feelings from the case, but I've failed to apprehend the Vigilante.

"As sure as we can be without an expert," Jeremiah says. He is shaking this new agent's hand, but I freeze.

On first appearance, the agent looks so bland that I'm sure I'm mistaken. Slick dark hair, thick-rimmed glasses that cover a boring pale face. In the morning light, it's obvious that he's a fed. The suit he wears fits poorly, and his stature is one of borrowed authority. I'm sure that the spark of recognition is flawed until he moves to shake my hand. The graceful walk that has a hitch of a limp if you look hard enough.

He looks different in this moment than he had last night, but familiarity makes my stomach revolt. The limp handshake we share irritates me, and I break contact too soon. Noticeably soon.

"I'm Special Agent Bradley. It's good to properly meet you, Special Agent Michaels. We didn't have the opportunity to exchange names upon our previous meeting." Bradley looks casually to Lt. Eisenhower. "Can you direct me to the coffeepot? I rushed out this morning."

The lieutenant sniffs but they leave the room, the rookie leaves the box of folders. My face is on fire when I meet Jeremiah's questioning gaze. Embarrassment is a clawing nausea in me. The thick feeling is flavored with frustration and useless self-directed anger.

It takes a second, but Jeremiah's eyes go wide in surprise before he starts laughing. I control myself enough to not throw something at the old man.

"Him?" Jeremiah gasps out.

I close my eyes and pinch the bridge of my nose, trying to block out the rest of the world. "*Fuck.*"

Jeremiah stops laughing. "Do you want me to… talk to him?"

I glare at my partner. I'm sure there must have been a moment more embarrassing in my life, but I don't recall it.

"Ookay, message loud and clear. I mean… it's not like you slept with the guy."

No, I just know how Agent Bradley's cock tastes.

Deep breath. It doesn't matter.

Jeremiah's mouth twitches. I will never, ever, live this moment down. It doesn't matter.

"I'll go talk to him."

CHAPTER 4

***

Agent Bradley is alone at the coffeepot, stirring in sugar methodically, but he looks up as I approach.

I know my blush is evident because my face burns, but this conversation has to happen. I will stay calm. I will coolly set the ground rules for us working together.

All of my good intentions go out the window when I see the gleam in Bradley's eyes.

"You knew who I was," I whisper. My face has been all over the news. Everyone knows about the terrible Ice Queen who is going after the Vigilante. Especially everyone in law enforcement.

"I thought you knew who I was too."

"You think I invite coworkers to bar storerooms on the regular?"

"I thought you wanted to talk about the case."

I rear back at that. "When did you figure it wasn't about the case? When I dodged your kiss or went down on my knees?"

No one is around to overhear us.

"I did say we should stop," he says.

"But you didn't stop me."

"I wasn't aware that I had to exert physical force to stop a sexual advance."

Shame cuts through my anger. I'm stunned to silence, blinking. Had I read the signs wrong?

Bradley looks at me, calm and cool before looking down in a way that communicates embarrassment. "I'll admit that I may have gotten caught up in the moment. I could have been more communicative."

"I didn't..." I'm having a hard time voicing the question.

"Ah, no. I was more than a willing party even if I didn't consent vocally."

We stand in painful silence before I break it. "I just wanted to tell you that it won't happen again, and we should try our best to make sure it doesn't impact the case."

It sounds weak now that I say it out loud.

Agent Bradley nods with a shrug. "The job is what's important."

I nod back, awkward now. Someone approaches, and we both turn toward Jeremiah.

"Time to go, kids. We've got another scene."

CHAPTER 5

Evelyn

It's a warehouse again. This time the casualty isn't from a different precinct.

Lt. Eisenhower meets us at the scene. He's white with an anger that brims under his surface but is appearing to keep calm, even after a tech drops something. His restraint is admirable.

Jeremiah and I rode together while Bradley followed in his own rental. Having three agents investigating is going to require some coordination. Jeremiah and I almost always shared a car, but more resources aren't something we'll ignore.

Eisenhower nods as we approach. "Officer Eric Miller didn't show up for his shift this morning. We got the call at ten. He's wearing his uniform but didn't work last night."

"When does our timeline begin?" Jeremiah asks.

"He lives ten minutes from here. His wife said that he left this morning at about seven-forty a.m. I informed her on my way here. I left an officer for when you want to interview her." The lieutenant's voice cracks.

Informing loved ones is a practice in ripping out your own heart. They don't care that we would give them the bloody organ just to stop them from screaming. They just don't want to hear the news we bring.

"And the identity confirmation?" I ask.

"Miller was a kid from my neighborhood before he entered the academy." The lieutenant's eyes are haunted.

I swallow. "I'm sorry for your loss, lieutenant."

The haunted look in the lieutenant's eyes morphs into one of fury. "We are going to get this fucker," he stops, trying to control his emotions before continuing. "I will admit that I didn't care about the Vigilante, the information made public after each time he struck showed the type that he targets. But Miller, Miller was a good man."

The confession of the previous unspoken belief is a reminder that none of us are unbiased individuals. I wish we could be unbiased, but I've never met anyone without flaws.

"We'll get him." My soft reply doesn't take away from the hard conviction of my words. The lieutenant looks at me, as if to pass judgment on my soul, and something he sees makes his shoulders ease.

"Just let us know what you need. Until then we'll run the scene as usual."

Our role is of a consulting nature. Many times, we do our own interviews, but we are really just an outside force looking in. Lt. Eisenhower continues organizing, and the time has come to see what the killer has left us. We duck under crime scene tape into a world of violence and blood.

Agent Bradley moves so silently I forget his presence until he speaks. "Did the murders yesterday happen in the morning as well?"

"As far as we can figure, until we get the report from the medical examiner, he acted in the early hours of the day. From the missed check-in of Officer Kerry and Officer James, we clock that time from three to five a.m.," I answer. It's in the preliminary report I sent, but that must not have made it to Agent Bradley's email. "You got here earlier than we thought."

"I was already in the area. About an hour north when I got the call."

The time for small talk is done and I force myself to look at the body as we approach. I've never seen one actually hung up. Usually, the body has already been collected by the time Jeremiah and I get to the scene. The photos are gruesome, but seeing it in real life… horrendous doesn't even start to cover it.

The only reason Jeremiah and I were able to be on the scene before the blood dried yesterday is that we were already in the area revisiting some past leads. This scene is fresh.

Officer Miller's body hangs from a noose around his neck. I course correct. The victim. I start to categorize the details separately so that the white noise in my ears doesn't overwhelm me. I will not vomit.

The rope is an ugly old thing, blackened on one side, that loops up around a crane hook before being tied off at a railing. The knot looks like it required expertise. I skip over the victim's face; the forensic report will be more knowledgeable about the body's appearance than I will be.

The victim's uniform is dirty. His right side shows streaks of dust and scrapes to the fabric. I walk around, the same dragging pattern continues on the victim's back. There is no clear indication if death occurred prior to hanging or after.

The slash across the victim's torso fits the gutting pattern of previous victims. The parts dangling from the incision have me blinking. I focus on breathing slowly from my mouth, but the air has a taste that brings to mind poorly disposed organ meat. I crave mouthwash or anything strong so the taste doesn't linger after we leave the scene.

"The knot looks professional," Jeremiah calls from his position next to the railing. His solid voice pulls me from reacting visibly. Becoming jaded to situations like this is a common thing in our line of work. But everything related to the Vigilante has me feeling like a raw nerve, exposed and sensitive.

Maybe I'm losing a taste for this work after all.

"The rope looks like something that came from this location. Do you think this is purely convenience or that the unsub knew the rope was here beforehand?" I ask no one in particular.

"What did he use at the scene yesterday?" Bradley still plays catch-up. I try to ignore that he looks pale.

"Chains," Jeremiah and I answer in unison.

I clear my throat. "The chains were stored, in sight, at the location."

The detail didn't indicate if they were used opportunistically or if the unsub had prior knowledge of them being there. We'll see if the same is true of this rope. If it's selective knowledge, that will limit the suspect pool from the general public.

The Vigilante is more careful than this copycat. He always uses the most generic rope that can be purchased from chain hardware stores. We'd already tried to track that purchase, and that trail didn't lead anywhere.

CHAPTER 5

Jeremiah

Neither of the kids look like they are handling the scene well. Adult kids. Teammates, that sounds better. As HR has tried to instill in me, just because everyone is younger doesn't mean I can call them kids.

Evie is okay with the terminology, but she has the capacity to forgive everyone for almost anything, except herself. And maybe some of the shittier people from her hometown.

Both Evie and Agent Bradley don't look too great about the gruesome scene in front of us. I'll ignore that I'm largely unaffected for now. Introspection is better left to a bottle, not a crime scene. Evie continues her visual inspection around the scene.

I lower my voice to Bradley. "You okay?"

The man's face is stark. He's trained it in a neutral expression, but his coloring keeps going white and sweaty. Bradley blinks rapidly, as if I've surprised him, before he nods and looks away from the body. "I just haven't seen many scenes like this one."

I nod in understanding. I worked as a police officer before joining the FBI. I've seen too many scenes like this. Blood, staged bodies, empty stares, bodies that barely look human.

Bradley glances over to Evie. "Is she—"

"She can do the job. If you have questions about her, you ask her," I cut him off. Too many times others have approached me about what Evie can or can't handle. She's one of the best damn agents I've worked with. She doesn't need me acting as her gatekeeper. I'll watch out for her, but I refuse to discuss her sensibilities with others.

"I'm sorry. That was… inappropriate." Bradley shakes his head.

Oh to make a list of the inappropriate things that have already happened in this case. Evie said that she and Bradley spoke about last night, but the tension between the two of them is still there. It's evident in the way Evie avoids looking at Bradley. And in the way Bradley's gaze appears as if he hasn't been watching her, but he has.

I preemptively regret what today will bring.

"I have a number of interviews to work with today. I'll start with the wife before moving on to finishing yesterday's interviews." I speak to Evie, "Eisenhower will deliver reports of the scene to you. I'll make sure to request that they track down where the rope is stored and who has access to it."

I'm the best with people, Evie is the best with organizing the details. With the extra manpower, we can do this quicker. I continue, "You should ride with Bradley back to the station and continue briefing him about the details."

Evie's face looks annoyed for a second before she wipes her expression. Her mouth still thins, but she nods. "That makes sense."

"Tomorrow we can do a full debrief after the scheduled autopsy. The ME got back to me and they are going to start on Officer James's autopsy at eight a.m."

I wouldn't stick her in this awkward situation if it wasn't the best situation.

CHAPTER 6
Evelyn

The man at the bar, my target, looks up when I approach. Something moves in his eyes that would have made me pause if I weren't so hard up. I don't waste time on conversation. I only need enough words to make the proposition.

"Want to join me in the storeroom?"

Bars always have storerooms. I'd cased it before committing to do this tonight. The man furrows his brow but stands, he's taller than I figured but this is my course now. I willingly turn my back to him and walk away.

I've been rejected a few times. I don't take it personally. There is nothing personal about this.

He follows me soundlessly. I turn to look at him when I get to the storeroom door and catalog that he has a limp, it's nearly unnoticeable.

The man goes into the storeroom, a mixture of cautiousness and confusion making his pace slow. This is the normal reaction from the men I pick. Always looking around to see if this was some sort of prank, but still willing to show up for the chance of something. I follow him in, leaving the door unlocked. We are two people who don't, and shouldn't, trust each other. I'll take being walked in on to the alternative.

Something about the way I move toward him has my mystery man opening his mouth. "We shouldn't do this."

That's the point.

I press my body to his. No matter what he says, he's interested. His cock is already heavy in his slacks.

The man leans in as if to whisper in my ear or kiss me, but I dodge him. Either action is more intimate than what I have in mind. I burn now, all my sense of cool logic gone.

I need to be dirty. It's the only way I'll be able to sleep tonight with the recent memory of the Vigilante in my ear.

I press my mystery man into the wall using my hands on his chest and tilt my head up.

"Stay."

Something about the way he looks now, with the shadows cast across his face, the intense way he watches me, niggles at the back of my mind that he's more than he appears. My heart rate picks up. There's a thrill that I rarely feel in this kind of transaction. I can't stop now even if I wanted to.

He could honestly just be dominant in the bedroom. That would be an interesting combination. Beta in the streets, alpha in the sheets. Not that we'll go anywhere near sheets. Whatever dominance this man feels, he listens to my order and I take a moment to feel the strain of his chest under the dress shirt he wears.

My mystery man watches carefully. I lean in and nip his neck, his scent is warm and welcoming. I slide a hand down the fabric and his chest swells when I trace his erection through his pants. He clutches some pipe on the wall behind him. His knuckles whiten when I reach his belt buckle.

I appreciate the appearance of restraint. The profile I use to pick my targets usually ensures that they aren't the type to hold my hair and choke me with their cock. I've only had one occurrence of it happening before. The guy was horrified with himself afterward. I didn't hate it, but I wasn't in danger of passing out because he barely lasted a minute.

When I drop to my knees, he exhales sharply. "Fuck."

I clench at his snarled tone. My bra feels too tight and I want to do things I've never let myself do on these types of liaisons, like unbutton my pants and touch myself. That would be escalation, and I refuse to let myself go there. My boundaries must stay in place.

I undo his pants; my sharp motions make his belt buckle jangle. The sound is loud and erotic in the small space. I draw out his cock and my eyes hood in anticipation as I grip him. He's sizable, one of the more attractive members I've seen, and I've seen many. The length and straightness of it will make it easier to swallow around it. No awkward bend or angles.

"So?" he asks. He sounds breathless even as he breathes deeply.

I've taken a moment too long in admiring his cock.

I raise my brows at him. "It will do."

I think he's going to laugh at that, but I take him in, and my mystery man lets out a string of curses.

Fuck. I moan. His cock is hot, and his salty taste hits my tongue in a way that has my toes curling. I hope this guy lasts longer than a minute. My tongue swirls around the shaft, wetting it. He punctuates his curse and I open my eyes to see him watching me, enthralled. I swirl my tongue again; it peeks out of my mouth for a moment and the man's whole body stiffens.

I smile around him before taking it deeper into my mouth. He moans and the throaty deepness has me wanting to rush this, take it all. I resist, taking my time to suck around the thickness. The bitterness of him increases with his precum and panting.

The situation has me in a daze. My body tightens impossibly, more affected than I ever have been. I squeeze my thighs together and squirm against my own arousal.

"Fuck. Are you as hot for this as I am? Do you like my cock so much you can't even keep still?"

His words are ridiculous, but I make a needy sound anyway. What a revelation; I didn't know I like dirty talk.

"You're so good at taking me. I think I'm going to come as soon as I hit the back of your throat. Because that's where I'm going, isn't it? You're going to take me down your throat."

I take him deeper in response and hum in the affirmative. I don't take him all in yet. This is the part I like the most, when he loses his mind. My body winds even tighter at his coaxing. The air is heavy.

"So fucking beautiful." *He sounds almost reverent. Something snaps in me at that. He's not supposed to sound awed. I repress my gag and force him all the way in, fucking into my swallowing throat. I gag anyway, not prepared for his length. My body contracts and I moan helplessly as the reaction pushes me higher, somewhere I don't go during this activity ever. I'm too far gone to stop it.*

"Fuck!" *he grunts. His hips rock forward to push deeper and I bob it in and out messily, making a desperate cry around him. My mind blanks and I come unexpectedly on a rush when he does. He shudders out in release and pulses in my mouth as I swallow.*

I'm dizzy, coming down from my climax and lack of air, when he pulls himself from my mouth, wiping various fluids from my face with his thumbs.

"Good girl," *he gasps.*

I snap out of my stupor at that and wipe my own mouth as I stand. I won't spend time worrying about my reaction. This was a one-time occurrence. I'm sure the next time I give in to the compulsion it will be back to my usual game. I nod to the stranger before leaving him against the wall in the storeroom, cock hanging out of his pants.

"Agent Michaels."

I startle at the sound of Agent Bradley's voice and want to hide my face at the lewd memory, but I don't. I look across the conference table and hope he doesn't notice the flush of my skin.

"Yes, Agent Bradley?" We just returned to the station. I sip a fresh cup of coffee, trying to get the taste of the crime scene out of my mouth.

"To make my profile, I'm going to have to go through all of the Vigilante crimes—"

I can't stop a bark of a laugh. Bradley looks confused. So very different from the restrained power I glimpsed last night. So different from the man that I climaxed for. *Stop.*

"That is going to be a lot of material." So many folders. "Let's gather the information for this crime while it's still business hours, and when people stop taking our phone calls, I can start to debrief you on the Vigilante cases."

"Calls?" Bradley doesn't sound thrilled, but the man has to know the monotonous procedure awaiting us.

"There are at least twenty shipping companies that use that warehouse location. The admins of those companies usually keep a list of individuals that work on site. I'll put some of Eisenhower's men on this too so we can get alibies and cross-check if any individuals knew the victims. Jeremiah should have a list of known enemies of the victims by end of day."

"Oh. That is… a lot."

Yes, it is. But it's leagues better than what Jeremiah has to do.

Jeremiah

Mrs. Angelica Miller's sobs lash me. Each tear a repeated injury to the same location, striking deeper every time. The pretty young woman would manage to stop crying for a moment before losing the fight and begin to sob again.

At least we are in her home and she doesn't need to worry about coworkers seeing us. The officer on duty informed me that Mrs. Miller works remotely as a graphic designer.

Officer Eric Miller's parents passed away in a car accident some years ago, and he only had an estranged brother left.

Mrs. Miller's mother is on her way to sit with her daughter so that she won't be alone after we're done with the interview. Which may take a while because of the crying. I don't rush the woman, even though I hear the clock ticking. Time presses down on my shoulders mercilessly.

Every minute wasted gives the Copycat time to cover possible trails. The Vigilante crimes keep us busy enough and those occur on a monthly basis. This copycat demonstrates no consistent timeline yet, and with the killing today happening at a busier hour of morning than yesterday makes me think that this killer is devolving—fast.

CHAPTER 6

Anyone with a badge, or even without one, is in danger of being the next victim.

There are photos on the mantle of Officer Miller and his wife together, beaming at the camera. Officer Miller had a promising future ahead of him according to the lieutenant and the man's record. He was well on his way to making detective.

This case hits close to me, ricocheting around my mind mercilessly. Would anyone call me if Marcus fell in the line of duty or would I have to find out from the news? My wounded heart keeps beating. My job still needs doing. Another person similar to my son could be dead by tomorrow.

"I-I think he said a man yelled at him from his car yesterday." Mrs. Miller gets the words out. The woman takes deep breaths.

My interest is piqued. "Like a threat?"

A sniffle. "He said it was a road rage thing."

I try my hardest not to look disappointed. "Was he in uniform at the time?"

Mrs. Miller nods but doesn't look positive.

"Did he say where?"

Officer Miller's vehicle had been found at the scene of the crime.

"I think he said it was near the station. I-I should have told him to report it."

"It's unlikely to be related, but I'll call it in to my partner just to be on the safe side." I make a note.

According to his wife, Officer Miller didn't have any enemies. I sit back to continue the interview, but Mrs. Miller's lip trembles and she breaks again. Weeping her heart out.

CHAPTER 7

Evelyn

Files and photos spread across my motel room floor. The amount of information overpowered the small motel coffee table earlier in the night. The table isn't all that's overpowered. Empty coffee cups and shed suit jackets attest that. It's just Bradley and me now, alone in my motel room.

Not the wisest decision.

This session had started properly back at the precinct with a light debrief on the information about the Vigilante details once businesses stopped picking up the phone. We could have spent hours on the Vigilante murders, and we're getting there.

Something about being in a near-empty station scatters concentration. As if being surrounded by empty desks makes the mind think that work should stop. We don't have time for the work to stop. Bradley needs to be fully debriefed to finish a copycat profile.

To combat the sensation of the station, Bradley and I brought the related files to my motel room. Stopping to get dinner on the way. Jeremiah had checked in briefly before heading to bed. It's now sometime past midnight, but I don't check the time.

CHAPTER 7

All checking the time will accomplish would be to call it a night to get sleep, and I already know I'm not going to sleep tonight. Every time I close my eyes, I see Officer Miller's bloated face or the headshot of Officer Kerry.

It's silly to avoid sleep, childish, but if I'm working, it's not really me avoiding sleep. Bradley also hasn't checked the time.

The spread of photocopied paper and photos are placed in chronological order. The accumulated knowledge about the Vigilante is intimidating. Trying to impart all of it to someone else feels like a futile task. How do you impart the impression that seeing the Vigilante's process evokes? But if anyone could intake the amount of information required, it's Agent Bradley. His focus throughout hours of work has been commendable.

In the motel room's yellow lighting and creeping shadows, that focus is different.

Some vain thing in me hopes I don't appear as ragged as Bradley does, but since I haven't been getting quality sleep for months, I doubt it. Bradley had initially raised a brow at my socked feet when I kicked off my shoes. But now, with his tie gone and shirt sleeves rolled up, we're in a contest for who looks the least professional while having to sit on the floor in front of the spread files.

So glamorous.

I'd vote that Bradley would win the contest. He has a habit of running his fingers through his hair in frustration. The effect is rather charming. The tousled hair gives him a roguish air that he hadn't possessed at the station. In this dingy motel room, long limbs sprawled, he almost resembles the man I approached in the bar. I veer my thoughts from that. Work. We're working.

Bradley isn't a different man than who I went down on my knees for, and I need to center my thoughts on anything else but that. My body is just confused by his attention. Bradley has listened to me go in-depth about the cases for hours. The focus so direct, like a physical touch.

It's rapturous not to have to work to keep his attention. I admit I can be long-winded about subjects and more than once have seen my listener's eyes glaze over. My mind wants to trick me into feeling like it's something special about me causing his focus, but that's ridiculous.

Agent Bradley picks up one of the earlier files.

"You've detailed almost all the past Vigilante crimes. Some things stay consistent, but there are enough variations to argue the current unsub could be him. How can you be so sure that this isn't the work of the Vigilante?" Curiosity edges his words.

I chew my lip. "The Vigilante doesn't target law enforcement and these murders are too… messy. The Vigilante works more methodically, these are rushed." I gesture at the photos in the spread even though I can see them with my eyes closed at this point. The scenes are precise, every detail planned out.

The Copycat murder scenes, by contrast, are rife with smears in the blood puddles under the hanging bodies with accompanying shoe prints leading away. As if the killer couldn't be bothered that the blood from the officers had soaked into his size ten sneakers.

"The killing of Officer James and Officer Kerry has all the signs of a crime of opportunity. Officer Miller appears to have been at random as well, just planned out better. The Vigilante targets specific individuals for what we assume is at least a month in advance in order to know the intricacies of their lives to get in and out as cleanly as he does."

My breath catches as I consider what I'm going to say. I had promised myself that I'd be open about my breach of conduct. To do anything different would endanger the case. I had put everything in the report to my supervisor, detailing my decision-making.

To keep this from Bradley would withhold pertinent information.

Agent Bradley is a by-the-books agent if I've ever met one. Even if that image seems to fade as the night wears on. *Will he judge me?* Of course he will. It doesn't matter. I still have to tell him.

"And... I called him." The confession hurts to say, scratches over the small part of my ego devoted to how other agents consider me. I clear my throat. "I called him at the first copycat scene."

Bradley stills. I've shocked him. What I've done is shocking. Silence hangs precariously between us before he breaks it.

"The Vigilante answered? He's never done that." Bradley's dark eyebrows knit together with suspicion.

"Well, he did when I called from my phone." I strive to sound calm. As if contacting a serial killer is a reasonable step. Get milk on the way home, don't run red lights, and contact the person that murdered eleven people, at least. The logical conclusion.

Silence returns between us, but Agent Bradley's stare makes breathing more difficult. His attention that had been so intoxicating before, now starts to flare warmth under my skin. An irritating warmth.

The edge of discomfort bites before Bradley looks away and shakes his head. My insides churn, oily and dark. It shouldn't matter what Bradley thinks of me, but somehow it does.

I'm tainted now, sullied. I've become the cautionary tale of a compromised agent. Nothing will ever be the same.

"You broke the rules; it makes me wonder how the Vigilante feels about that." Agent Bradley sets down the folder and removes his glasses in a considering motion as he inspects the frames before setting them on the coffee table. Everything about the situation starts to feel weighted, personal.

Confusion swirls down a drain. "What do you mean?"

"I wonder if he'll see you as some fallible being now. Before, only going on reputation, you were someone who always does the right thing. Some might even say saintly. Untouchable." He pauses and his words fall in the space between us, significant. "Obviously, he's fixated on you. You're the only point of contact he'll go through."

Bradley leans back against the couch and stares at me without his glasses. His eyes look black in the poor lighting. *What does he see?* The analytical way his gaze travels cuts through the image I project to the world. It's intimate.

He doesn't see past my façade. This moment is mere perception. My starved, sad soul searching for connections.

I try to reorder my mind by avoiding the dark eyes. *Business.* We are talking about business.

"You think that's why he sends the phones to my desk?" The topic is sticky, but I grab on to it with both hands. It shouldn't be a surprising statement that the Vigilante has fixated on me. The way he murmurs and the timbre of his voice over the phone tastes personal.

This is an easier topic to mull over instead of deciphering the shift of atmosphere in the motel room.

The air permeates my skin, sinking in and spreading a drugging laxness to my limbs. Agent Bradley shrugs in response.

"Your notes on the crime scene are in-depth, so focused and unerringly unbiased. Every single item is included. You make the report so honest that one can't see your influence at all. It makes me wonder, how do you feel about the Vigilante, Agent Michaels?"

He deepens his voice in a way that hints at suggestion, and shivers dance down my spine. My cheeks heat. Maybe he can't see me blush in this lighting. I analyze a patch in the motel wall to give my eyes somewhere else to go. This isn't business. This is dissecting my motivations with the flick of the scalpel.

Someone so observant is a double-edged sword. They see the things you don't want seen. Things that hurt when they surface.

"You should call me Evie."

What am I doing?

Agent Bradley breathes in my change in topic but keeps watching me.

"My friends call me Eugene." He sounds amused. The speculative glint in his eyes has me craving something I'll probably regret. I remember the taste of him from the night at the bar. The way my body responded when he spoke.

Would a dalliance really matter at this point? That bridge has already been crossed. The seductive way this conversation strokes over me like silk over skin is purposeful. The man in front of me doesn't try to hide his intention. He asks questions about the Vigilante, but he wants something else.

I'm inclined to give in. Something about the way he speaks calls to me in a way that rarely happens. A promise lies in the smooth cadence of his words.

"So, Gene, why are you looking at me that way?"

I get an eyebrow raise for the nickname, but I brazen it out. This is how I was before the specter of the Vigilante started haunting my days and nights. Direct and sharp, the resurgence of familiar traits is a relief, a homecoming if home were a place of comfort instead of where grief lay six feet deep.

"We should take a break." He ignores my question, definitely amused now. The moment stretches, an impending gravity sucking at my willpower. Gene extends the arm he had propped on the couch cushion behind him and I inhale at the soft stroke of his finger running down my neck to the collar of my dress shirt.

It's a testing of the waters.

Maybe in the light of day, I'll conclude that it's just the late hour that morphed the man in front of me from the bland agent to someone that stirs my emotions and body. Or maybe I'll ignore this memory altogether.

Curiosity for what Gene offers drags me along.

"Do you want to play a game, Evelyn?"

My eyelids go heavy at the delicious way Gene's voice lowers. I should be more wary instead of letting myself be lulled by him. Gene is a man with the power to cut me. But I'm so hungry for *this*.

He continues, "Just some harmless fun, I'm very curious and you're strung so tight, wanting. We could even have a safe word."

My brows rise and Gene's hand spreads over the back of my neck. The touch is a small one, but the searing sensation of it has me wanting to agree to play whatever game he desires.

"Is 'stop' not a good enough safe word?" I ask and bite back a moan when Gene's thumb digs into my neck, massaging a muscle there. My shoulders start to ease, melting into his touch.

Gene's smile is teasing. "Not usually, but for this 'stop' works just fine. So, do you say yes, Evelyn?"

My thighs tense at the knowing way my full name curves out of his mouth. My body is here for this game. The dream-like quality of my mind is willing.

"Yes."

The approval on Gene's face makes me want to agree multiple times over. Dangerous man.

"Tell me honestly, Evelyn, if the Vigilante were here, what would you do with him?" Gene's finger drags down my collar and flicks one of my shirt buttons open. "Arrest him?" The next button gives. "Let him go?"

My shirt is halfway open. Gene's hot hand touches the sensitive skin of my chest as he undoes another button. It hypnotizes me.

"Or fuck him?"

A knife bites past my surface and releases a slew of underlying emotion.

Rage combines with embarrassment and surges through me like a wildfire yielding only violence. It burns quick and hot, my back hits the ground and Gene holds my wrists above my head. My hands are shaped into angry claws that had struck out against the mental assault. The fire banks and I gasp in disbelief at my own actions. *Mercy*. I tried to assault a federal agent. *What the fuck is wrong with me?*

Gene's grin is wolfish.

"I know what the Vigilante would do if he were here." His words are accompanied with the snick of cold metal around my wrists, *handcuffs*. He's looped them around the couch leg, the carpet scrapes at my back. Fear bleeds through the blackened result of my rage.

Gene must sense my shift because he strokes the skin of my wrist and gazes at me intensely. "Do you want to keep going?"

My breath comes out shaky. That is the question, isn't it? Keep going, participate in a role-play where Gene is the Vigilante. I shouldn't. This is perverse. Something that would have disgusted me before my trek through the sleepless land of chasing this killer.

But the excitement that had thrummed through me during our earlier discussion hasn't fizzled. If anything, it feels as if every single nerve in me fires at this offer combined with the weight of his body over mine. It's all so reminiscent of when I wake, my body on edge of some mysterious sensation. Fear? Pleasure? Both?

"We shouldn't," I say.

Gene's mouth twists in a knowing way. "My impression was that doing what you shouldn't is what you like."

I flush hot. Thinking about the other night.

This light kink experience will be the only time I'll be able to imbibe in the forbidden fruit.

Later, I'll analyze my reactions to Gene's offer, but now he watches me patiently. Waiting for my consent now that he's revealed his intentions. I nod and Gene smiles slowly.

"Good girl. So brave."

I narrow my eyes at the term, and he chuckles, sitting up over me with the aura of a predator.

"The question, Evelyn, is if you can be tempted." Gene runs his hand up over my dress shirt, giving my breast a teasing squeeze.

I flush and pull at the cuffs; my wrists burn at the pressure in an exquisite way. I don't even care that there will be marks tomorrow. Gene's motivations for this game are a mystery, but I let myself ease into the scene as he continues his dark words.

"Or will you be my very own saint? Will I kneel before you to beg for protection, redemption for my past mistakes?" He runs his lips up my neck while deftly finishing unbuttoning my shirt. The fabric opens to expose my plain bra.

So many things in my life are plain, uninteresting, but not what's happening. This is interesting. The face Gene makes when he sits back and looks his fill is both gratifying and spikes my anticipation. His expression is so open, his appreciation avid and aroused.

I don't want a drawn-out game. The sooner this is over with, the sooner I can get back to forgetting I wanted this. To forgetting I need this.

"Condoms are in my suitcase," I pant.

Gene goes still, his eyes narrow to laser focus on my face. "Tell me, Evelyn, do you do this often? Run from city to city following the Vigilante and let your coworkers fuck you along the way? Choke on the cock of strangers?"

My rage is icy. The lines between reality and fantasy blur.

"Fuck you! You don't know anything about me." I thrash, but Gene pins me heavily with his weight. I can't even kick him with him lying between my legs. The cuffs dig deeper into my wrist. His movements feel charged with more than lust as he bites my shoulder.

Everything in me tenses in rebellion to the pain before I melt into a whimper. I should hate this. This play that borders on violence and danger, but I can't make myself do anything but feel the rawness of it. Every sensation is sharper, brighter.

"You'd be surprised how much I know about you; how much I can tell from your every reaction."

Gene punctuates his words by pulling down my bra with rough movements, exposing my breasts. He slides a hot hand over my exposed skin, engulfing my sensitive breast and squeezes. I gasp and my hips buck. The dangerous man over me keeps talking.

"How much I could tell from you forcing yourself to choke around me. Do you know how many times I had to jerk off to be able to sleep after that? I knew before I came here you were dangerous to me. So bright, so beautiful. Goddamn immaculate. But I didn't know you could destroy a man with that perfect saintly mouth." Gene snarls, "I didn't know you'd get on your knees for just anyone. What a fucking contradiction you are."

Slut, whore, dirty thing.

My emotions are untraceable. Different flashes of arousal, shame, pride. Gene looks as devout as any sinner seeking redemption as he massages both of my breasts now, pinching my nipples hard. I cry out. Heat flows through me, each sharp point bringing me higher.

"My saint. I don't care who you've sucked, you're mine."

I want to deny it. Tell him he's wrong. But my mouth won't open. The lies that lay on my tongue refuse to be expressed.

"I can tell how much you want this." Gene rocks his hips into the cradle of my legs. I shudder in bliss at the sensation of his hard cock. The image of being taken so thoroughly has a small sound escaping my mouth. I trap my plea in my throat.

"But I'm not in a giving mood tonight." With those crisp words, Gene slides down my body, teasing my bare skin on his way. A light lick to a nipple, the graze of teeth to the skin across my rib. Light touches that taunt, tantalize, and contribute to the impossible slickness between my thighs.

Mesmerized, I watch as he unbuttons my pants. The hard yank of them makes me gasp as Gene pulls them completely off my legs, taking my panties with the pants. Leaving me bare.

The cold air hitting my wet sensitive parts is a shock. Gene lets out a helpless groan. He lifts one leg, hand under my knee, spreading me.

"Already so wet for this. How terrible of you, Special Agent Evelyn Michaels, getting wet for an atrocious criminal."

My face, already hot from shame at being splayed open like this, heats further from the way he says my full title. Exactly the way the Vigilante does.

The way Gene looks at me has my body craving to arch and legs to tense. He looks hungry.

Gene's eyes flick to mine and I watch as he unbuttons his own shirt, discarding it, then pulling off the undershirt. He's watching my facial expression as he bares himself, but it doesn't stop me from reacting. There is a hardness to Agent Bradley that hadn't been evident before. Gene is all sinew and strength. With the way he dominates, the effect is overpowering.

Gene must like what he sees on my face because his smile is a wicked thing. The smile brings to mind dark fairy tales and nursery rhymes told to young girls so they don't end up in situations like this. It's too late for me. I've wandered into the dark woods and the big bad wolf closes in.

As Agent Bradley, Gene blends in; a bland face among other bland faces. But in this moment, he's singular, all power and will. Which is the act? *Do I care?* All that exists at this moment is what is happening between us.

I'm not helpless. I can get away if I want. A childhood of being locked in places I didn't want to be means that I keep a selection of lock picks in my watch band at all times. I don't reach for them though. I want this scene to play out with the added fear of being restrained.

Gene lowers himself until his breath warms my most intimate place. A tease. He kisses my inner thigh. I gasp as he gives a single lick up through my folds. The man groans in a way that has my lower muscles clenching as he licks me again, slower, savoring.

This isn't pleasure, it's punishment. Every touch of his mouth burns and makes me writhe. The confusing part is that it's also pleasure.

The conundrum makes my mind spin and jump. The moan I've been trying to keep in breaks free. Gene grunts at the sound and dives into the task of tonguing me until I can't keep track of the pathetic noises I make. They're numerous. My body isn't my own. Under this man's tongue, I reel and wind higher and higher until I tense in the beginnings of an orgasm.

Gene pulls away.

"No!" I sob, so worked up I don't care how I sound.

"Shhh, I've got you." Gene's tone isn't reassuring. His eyes burn and his mouth is erotically wet. The sight drives my ache higher. He touches me though. I sigh as he runs his thumb through my wetness before circling my clit. His touch is so soft I whimper and squirm. Not able to drive me into the ecstasy I skirt.

"I could keep you like this all night. So goddamn beautiful, writhing around my fingers and tongue. I never thought I could reduce a saint to this. I thought you'd be incorruptible, but you're really just starving to be touched. Aren't you, Evelyn?"

All night? Hell no. I release the cuffs easily with some covert movements. I refuse to let this man torture me, sensual or otherwise. Gene watches his thumb stroke through my pussy. I use that distraction to my advantage and grapple for the high ground. The man is larger and stronger, but I have some training and the element of surprise on my side.

I end up straddling his hips after cuffing his wrist to the leg of the coffee table.

A look of uncertainty crosses Gene's face before he barks a laugh, he stops, breathless. He gives me a heated look that strikes me to my core. My desperate weeping core. I want to use my advantage to fill myself with his cock, but a sadistic streak in me craves returning the punishment.

"Not a saint after all but an avenging angel." Gene's voice is husky, and a glow of admiration and worship shows in his eyes. "What will my avenging angel do with me now that you've caught me, if only one-handedly?"

My avenging angel. The term is both hard-edged and soft. It's a term that is going to linger in my mind long past this hookup. The smart thing to do would be to stop this now. Keep any other stains from my psyche.

Be logical, Evie. But I can't. My heart races, and excitement is a living animal inside me, clawing for this risk. All the anonymous hookups prior are shadows compared to the vivid dark eyes that watch me.

Gene's hard cock pulses against me. The man below me seems as thrilled with my rough handling as I am with his role-play. We both groan when I give in to the temptation and grind myself against his fabric-covered hardness.

"If I cuffed both of your hands, you wouldn't be able to touch me. I want you to touch me. Though, I might have to arrest you in the end anyway."

This vantage point allows me to see Gene's reactions. The tops of his cheekbones flush a ruddy color compared to his pale complexion.

I take my time admiring Gene's chest, running a hand down his bare skin, feeling the cords of muscles tense under my touch. The light glints off of a necklace he wears. Without thinking, I run a finger over it. It's a medallion, I make out a figure with wings on it.

"You're religious?" I ask.

"Just in my memories."

Too close. I mentally retreat. We aren't here to make small talk. I let the texture of his skin distract me. When I get to his lower stomach, my hand runs across to the scarring that starts on his side and travels along the top of his hip bone before disappearing under his pants. I remember the limp. The injury looks old.

"Am I not as pretty as you expected?" he challenges. It's surprising to find something the enigmatic man appears to be sensitive about. It's a tiny break in our scene, but it isn't in me to ignore the insecurity completely.

I keep my voice cool. "If you really want to know, I'm wondering if I should ask for a doctor's note. I'd hate to break you from being too rough."

CHAPTER 7

The breath shudders from Gene, going shallow. "*Fuck. Evelyn.*"

Gene's hips tilt under me and he grits his teeth. The darkness probably hides my smile.

"That's Special Agent Evelyn Michaels to you."

"I want to be inside you, Special Agent Evelyn Michaels. I want to fill you up with my cock until you scream for me. Special. Agent. Evelyn. Michaels."

He's too good at playing this part. His words have me rocking against him again, making us both shudder this time. I move my hand over to his belt buckle now, letting my nails scratch across his lower stomach in a way that makes him hiss.

The way I yank his belt and pants open is reminiscent of last night and the underlying memories has my breath coming faster. Wanting no obstacles, I pull down his pants and boxers past his knees. A satisfied sigh comes from me when his cock is free. It's just as nice looking as he was when I first had my mouth on him.

I sit back and remove my open dress shirt and bra. Gene's eyes travel over my naked body and I wait, enjoying watching him.

I trace Gene's scar lightly; it goes all the way down to his knee. Like he had to be put back together again. I raise an eyebrow.

"I don't care if you break me," he says. Fervent.

My lips curl, my mind on other things. "I'm going to taste you again."

Gene's eyes widen in a way that would have made me laugh if my body wasn't on fire.

I need to torment this man. Take out every frustration that has been building since the hunt for the serial killer began. Every sleepless night, pointed question from the media, and growly phone call that made me feel indescribable things.

"Evelyn." The danger in Gene's voice is dark, swirling around me, bathing me. A commanding note sounds through it as if he is still in control of this situation. "I won't last long if you take me in your mouth."

Well, he's honest at least. But this is something I can draw out. If not, I'm not concerned. A ravenous nature hums under Gene's skin; he's going to need more than a hot mouth to satisfy him.

"Well then, you have some motivation to figure out a way out of those cuffs. Don't worry, I'll give you the time you need. Just as much mercy as you gave me should be fair." I almost sound sweet.

It contrasts with the ruthless way I swirl my tongue around the head of his cock. Gene's head falls back and his low groan makes me wetter than I already am. I take him into my mouth and the muscles in his thighs tighten under my hands as I taste salt.

Gene's free hand falls into my hair, grasping, pulling at the roots. He doesn't stop me from slowly sucking him deeper, but the presence of the barely contained dominance has my hips shifting.

I lose myself in the sensation of his cock in my mouth and the sounds Gene makes. Intervals of gasps and moans. *I could come just from listening to him.* I don't want to come feeling so empty though.

The first time I take Gene to the edge and stop, he throws his head back with an expression that I'd describe as agony. He hisses out a curse before glaring at me, holding my hair tightly in his fist. That look almost has me moaning. A promise of retribution for my actions.

I murmur sweet nothings and stroke my hands up his thighs in a poor form of comfort until Gene's muscles unclench. When I suck him back into my mouth, Gene snarls curses at me and I hear the handcuff pull tight against the coffee table leg. He's in a bad way.

"Goddammit, Evelyn."

The tension on my hair isn't enough to keep me from taking him deep. Aiming to take him to the edge again.

A crash sounds before my back hits carpet, wrists held over my head, again. Gene's body collides against my sensitized one, and he mercilessly thrusts inside me.

I cry out in relief and ecstasy at the stretch of it. The initial resistance of my body trying to take his forces a groan from both of us. His next thrust has his hips meeting mine and I gasp.

I wrap my legs around him and a hard drive scoots me against the carpet, roughening my skin.

Gene moves his arms to cage me, trap me, so he can fuck me into the carpet instead of against it. The press of his hard cock inside me is bliss even as the harsh way he moves into me borders on pain. I sink my nails into his arms.

This is a reckoning for everything I've ever done, everything he's done. A sacrifice for the altar of our crimes.

Words fall from Gene's lips and ratchet my sensations higher. "Fuck, Evelyn, you feel so good. Everything I ever wanted. Goddamn angel."

My back arches and I cry out when my climax hits me. It shouldn't be such a surprise that I'm coming so soon. The role-play has had me on edge since the beginning. The world ends for a split second as my body and mind shatter. The sensation of clenching on a cock while orgasming so unfamiliar of late that the experience sears me, brands me.

Gene powers into my body with fierce, helpless motions until his pace falters. "I'm going to—fuck!"

The last part sounds panicked as Gene lurches out of me, wet warmth covers my stomach. We both gasp as if we've run a marathon. I ease my nails from the man's skin, seeing the angry half-moon marks I leave on him.

I laugh, breathless as the hair from Gene's bowed head tickles my face. At my laugh, his lips touch my throat for a second before he moves off of me. The wetness between my legs is probably too much to have just been from me. I'm having a hard time caring in my current state.

I haven't felt this light in years. Back when I thought being good at my job would earn me acceptance from my respectable colleagues. Back before every groove I hit in my life felt like a well-worn rut. I float and the sensation is beautiful.

I'm too busy coming down to notice Gene until he presses a warm washcloth between my legs. The intimate action has me feeling unbelievably shy. Yes, this man had been inside me, but we haven't even kissed.

"Gene, you don't need to—"

He interrupts me with a frustrated sound in the back of his throat. "Just let me take care of you for a second, Evelyn."

I'm speechless as I watch him gently clean his release from my stomach. I've never experienced a moment like this one, having a lover wash my body. It's funny that as surprising as the perverse role-playing had been, this action is the one that shocks me.

I might need counseling.

Gene throws the soiled cloth into the tub before picking me easily off the carpet. I scrabble against his naked chest before wrapping my arms around his neck.

He had kicked off his pants and now walks around the room naked as if he owns the place.

"What are you doing?" My voice sounds shrill. No one has carried me like this since early childhood.

The overturned coffee table solves the mystery of how Gene had gotten free of his restraint. He hadn't, the cuff still hangs on one wrist. Most of the files on the floor still looked intact.

Gene carries me over to the bed in the room before pulling the covers back and dropping me on the cool sheets. "Going to bed, it's a thing that humans need to do."

He slides a hand up my wrist until he gets to my watch. It's a thicker band style that looks unfeminine, but the utility of it can't be argued as he helps himself to a selection of different picks I keep there. I silently watch him as he expertly removes the handcuff before sliding the pick back in its place on my wrist.

When he clicks off the light and slides into the bed with me, I find my voice again. "What are we going to do, cuddle?"

Warm arms wrap around me, turning me onto my side, and his naked body spoons mine. My mouth opens and my lips tremble. Actually, my whole body is shaking. *When had that started?*

"Adrenaline comedown. Breathe, angel." He massages my shoulder and I try to take a deep breath.

The heat of Gene's body against mine is so comforting that I let myself be handled. Gradually the shaking stops, but he keeps running his hands up and down my body in a wonderfully soothing way. I soften. Almost falling asleep with this stranger, but he speaks.

"We didn't use the condoms... I'm clean, but I don't think I pulled out soon enough." Gene seems pained by the admission. Guilty. I hadn't raised any objections in the heat of the moment and honestly, I don't regret it. Not really. It's the hottest thing I've ever experienced.

"I'm clean," I say. I get tested all the time. Oral sex is still sex.

Gene waits for something else. His body coils in tension the longer he waits. Is this the moment he expects me to say that I'm conveniently on birth control? I haven't been in a relationship since before going to Quantico. I have the urge to roll my eyes but shrug instead, voicing my own thoughts on the matter.

"It's probably not the right time of the month."

When had I even last had a period? That's probably something to figure out. I abuse my body with too many late nights and missed meals for it to run on anything as convenient as a cycle.

Gene's body relaxes behind mine and I snicker.

He huffs at my mirth. "I wouldn't want to damage your career with something so unplanned."

That's actually kind of a sweet sentiment, if a little late. I do appreciate it. As useless as it is.

"My career is plenty damaged without a surprise pregnancy. It's just a matter of time." I start to drift again. I haven't slept through the night in so long, it's no surprise that I'm so sleepy. The pillow talk comes so naturally with Gene holding me.

"What? Why? Your record speaks for itself. You've never failed to solve a case."

Gene's surprise warms my heart. It's nice to have someone more than just Jeremiah on my side when it comes to work. *Fuck it.*

I turn toward Gene and push our position until I can lay against his chest. He moves slowly but accommodates me. I don't know when I'll next be able to be in bed with a man, so I might as well enjoy the best parts of cuddling while I do. His heart beats under my ear, the small intimacy has my eyes stinging but I blink away the sensation before I start.

"You can't be naïve enough to think that makes me any friends in the Bureau. On paper and to the public that all looks great, but you're not asking the right questions. You should be asking why I was put on the Vigilante case? Or why it has always had a fraction of the manpower a case of this body count should?" I hum. "A perpetrator loved by the public vs. an agent with a high rate of solved cases."

I pause until I feel Gene's body tense in understanding. Feel him solve the puzzle I've laid out.

"My career is all but over if I do get the Vigilante. Death by public opinion and the Bureau is still a bureaucracy. And I'm damned by my superiors if I don't. A real unwinnable situation, but I always get my man."

Sleep is coming for me. It makes my voice have a slight slur. It's a joy to fall asleep like this, with Gene stroking my back.

It's also wonderful to verbalize the issues I'm having with my work. Jeremiah and I both know the score without talking it over. Confiding in someone else, having them get angry on my behalf, is validating.

I'm drifting when Gene speaks again, "Why did you call him, Evelyn?"

I sigh. *Why can't my body pillow let me sleep?* I'm so blissed out from the earlier orgasm that my mouth answers his questions. I'm not awake enough to try to filter my speech. To keep things secret.

"There is always the possibility that this killer is just warming up. That those officers were the opening act to the grand finale." A weight lifts with every word I say. Finally telling my personal hypothesis to someone. Gene runs a hand up my neck, starting to massage my scalp. The strong fingers over the sensitive areas is nirvana.

"Everything about the way this killer regards the Vigilante is personal. Idolatry at its finest. So, what target is most associated with the Vigilante? What person's death would most serve the actual Vigilante?"

Gene takes a breath before whispering, "You. You're the media sensation. He'll target you."

I hum in agreement. I'm being rather flippant about the idea of my own death, but there has always been a risk to the job I do. This risk is just more direct. Relaxation pulls me down and I forget to keep talking until Gene tugs on my hair a little. I still haven't answered Gene's question, annoying body pillow.

"Honestly, I might not get out of this alive. I can be careful, stay armed, but the possibility is always there that I'll be the next body swinging on a rope. I didn't want to feel… so alone. It's stupid, but if I don't make it out of here, I wanted to hear from him just one more time. I never meant for this. For you to come…"

My body pillow goes stiff. My sleepy brain recedes, and I try to figure out what I just said. I stiffen.

Oh shit. Fuck.

My admission hangs in the dark. My heart starts to pound. I despondently notice that the heartbeat of the man holding me doesn't change. Dread makes it hard to think. I haven't prayed since I was a child. It hadn't done a lot of good then. Still, I send a hope into the universe that he will laugh off my words.

Gene's fist clenches in my hair, holding me immobile.

CHAPTER 8

Evelyn

"You knew?" The Vigilante's voice drops into the gravelly range I'm familiar with. The same gravelly range he spoke in while inside of me.

I'm in danger. Before I'd stupidly opened my mouth, the Vigilante wouldn't have hurt me. Not for any sentimental reasons. He doesn't target law enforcement and it would have ruined his cover. Now, now it's a question of self-preservation. Will he leave me alive with what I know?

I have to get away. My body explodes into movement, trying to ignore the pull of my hair, but the Vigilante anticipates my fight. He flips us, easily pinning me to the bed. He catches my wrists before I can try and claw his eyes to escape.

The Vigilante's other hand wraps around my throat, giving a light squeeze to show how easily he can block my airways.

"I asked a question, Agent Evelyn Michaels."

"It sounded more like a statement." My voice is soft, careful.

The Vigilante curses under his breath and squeezes my throat again.

"I suspected," I whisper.

It's dark, but moonlight edges the man above me. Agent Bradley is gone, the man with his hand around my throat has an intense demeanor and eyes that glitter with frustration.

"And you still invited me into your bed?" He sounds stunned.

This is—awkward. How to explain something I don't understand myself?

"Would you have rather I arrested you?"

The Vigilante's hand tenses around my throat, threatening. The fear sparks other sensations and my body arches. My face heats in embarrassment when the Vigilante eases the pressure on my throat with a jerk of surprise.

"God, you're a little fucked-up." He doesn't sound disgusted, more confused, and maybe a little intrigued.

Just bury me now. This has gone from awkward to humiliating. I still burn. Even the confirmation of his identity doesn't have my senses returning.

My laugh is humorless. "Don't I know it."

"What am I supposed to do with you?" The words aren't taunting. The fearsome Vigilante appears at a loss for how to handle the situation. Which, hopefully, means he won't kill me. Comforting.

"I don't know anything about you. This truce we have could last through this case before we have to be on opposite sides again." We both know I'm lying. I know a lot: his face, his scent, that he has an old injury that would have required surgery.

Our naked bodies still press into each other. Is that the reason why he's hard? My hips rock without me thinking about it and the Vigilante takes a breath.

CHAPTER 8

"Stop trying to distract me," he says.

I still. A distraction. That would have been a really good idea. A better idea than the fact that his body against mine steals all my good sense.

The Vigilante keeps his hand on my throat and releases my wrists, starting to move above me in the direction of the lamp but freezes when his positioning causes his thigh to grind against my pussy and I whimper. My wetness is obvious. Painfully obvious.

He clears his throat and my blush becomes even hotter. *Fuck.*

"Don't tease me, Evelyn." His request sounds like a prayer. "We can turn on the lights and talk about what options I'm going to give you."

It all sounds very responsible. My body doesn't want to be responsible and the body above me is tight, hard with arousal, rough with frustration.

"And if we don't turn on the lights?"

The grip around my throat is more a cradle now. My hips shift against his thigh, the friction against my tender parts is so much but not enough. The Vigilante brings his face next to mine, the brush of his exhale tickles my lips.

"Don't invite me back inside you knowing who I am, Evelyn. What I've done." His tone is forbidding.

"I let you inside before, knowing."

His mouth meets mine in the dark. The kiss is startlingly sweet at first. His mouth opens and his taste is minty, coffee, and my own taste. The excitement that kindles in me from tasting my own wetness on this man is primal. I'm sensitive everywhere. His teeth scrape my lip and I want to sob.

The kiss goes on and on. The Vigilante drinks from me as if I'm communion wine, as if I'm his only chance at absolution, and I let him. I follow him toward whatever oblivion he's chasing. I moan when our tongues slide against each other. I claw at his chest, needing everything.

The kiss breaks and I gasp, "Please."

Shame slithers through me and sparks my arousal, like it always does. The Vigilante isn't going to kill me this minute, but the unspent adrenaline might. I squeeze my thighs around the heft of his body, wanting him to thrust inside me again. Wanting all the things I shouldn't ever want.

He tears himself from me in a confusing rustle of sheets. I try and reach into the dark but don't catch him before he's out of the bed. A whine is in my throat. I'm bereft, a gaping space of painful emptiness. Sounds are happening in the room. In my mind's eye, I see the Vigilante grabbing his clothes as if to leave. Panic rises in my throat.

"No—"

The Vigilante interrupts me when he climbs into the bed again with the distinctive crinkle of a foil packet. I sigh a breath of relief before gasping in surprise when he pulls me to straddle him. His latex covered erection is hot against my pussy. There is enough moonlight to give me a striking visual of him looking up at me.

The Vigilante's intense face almost looks reverent before his mouth opens, spilling filth.

"Ride me, angel, work for this cock that can't seem to get hard for anyone but you. If you do arrest me, I'll spend the rest of my life remembering the way you begged me to fuck you and say prayers of gratitude for the opportunity."

His words leave me breathless, but my body moves to comply. I rub the head of his cock through the wet mess of my folds before sinking myself slowly down. My flesh, sore from the frantic fucking prior, stretches around the hardness and I wince. There is no stopping this though and the pain just makes me bear down harder. I pace my body with small pulses. Easing the hardness deeper.

"That's it, take it all, punish me with your cunt. You snap those handcuffs on me and all I'll be able to think about is how hot you felt around me. How pretty your cunt looks with me inside."

"Don't. Talk." I can't handle thinking about arresting this man when he's filling me up. The Vigilante gives a hollow laugh but groans as the roll of my hips brings me down to the base of him.

The stretch of my body around his is tight and satisfying. I tense around him and his hips pump upward, the force of it has me panting. I place my hands against his chest before starting the up and down motions of riding his cock.

The Vigilante's eyes watch his cock disappear inside me and reappear wet. "Fuck, Evelyn. So goddamn perfect. You think you're an ice queen but you're so hot on the inside. I don't know how I lasted as long as I did without the condom."

My body sets the pace. I mindlessly move and gasp. The orgasm coming for me isn't as cataclysmic as the one on the floor was, but the Vigilante moves his thumb to my clit, pressing against it in a way that teases. The waves of an oncoming climax start to beat through me.

Right when I'm going to start really fucking myself on him, he uses his grip on my hips to stop me.

"Easy. Not so fast. Feel me inside you."

I whimper but let him stroke me from the inside and out, trapped between his cock and thumb. The man moves me in a sensuous way that has my climax breaking, and breaking, with no end. The rocking of our bodies building the waves of pleasure in me to a slow but high crescendo. My body stiffens, and I cry out.

The Vigilante's voice weaves around me, through me.

"That's it, angel. So beautiful when you come. I could die a happy man after just seeing your face with me inside you."

I'm begging by the time the Vigilante lets himself fuck into me with abandon. The rough smacking of our bodies driving me high again and when he shouts, my mind goes blank again, feeling the kick of his cock coming inside me.

I fall forward on a sigh. Gene-not-Gene's lips brush my forehead in what could have been a kiss before he moves me off of him. We both make a sound when he slides out of me. He cleans up for the second time tonight before climbing back into bed.

I don't complain about the intimacy of our bodies this time. This is something that will never happen again. I'll relish the warmth of this man's body for now. There are questions in my mind, one flies free before I can hold it back.

"Why did you come here?"

Will he answer? I don't bother asking if Eugene is his real name. To think about continuing the hunt for this man while his sweat cools on my skin is blasphemy.

"You called. How could I not come?"

After nine months circling each other, that isn't really an answer. I start to prop myself up to question him more thoroughly, but the Vigilante hugs my body to his, keeping us in our spooning position. I huff.

"Go to bed, angel, hard discussions can wait until morning."

My eyelids are heavy. I like when he calls me *angel* too much. I concede the battle, for now, and fall asleep against the naked body of my enemy.

CHAPTER 9

Evelyn

The light is what wakes me. With my awful sleep schedule, it's rare to sleep until the sun is out. Dawn light spills into the room through the cracks in the curtains. I blink, the room feels unfamiliar in the light of day. *Empty.*

I sit up in bed and look around. I'm alone. The sheets cool beside me.

Something unwieldy and terrible catches in my throat. It takes a moment to make myself breathe past the clawing feeling of inappropriate disappointment.

Waking up alone is not a surprise. Of course, he's gone. It would be stupid for the man to stick around after all the confessions we'd made in the dark. *Why does my heart hurt?*

I allow the pain to echo through me for a minute. Let it touch every weak part of my psyche before I exhale and clench my hand in a fist. A list. I need to make a list of things to do. There is still a copycat killer out there. After we catch him, I'll focus on apprehending the man who called me beautiful.

First thing on the list: clean up the damn files. The real copycat expert will probably show up soon, won't that be a fun conversation to have with Jeremiah, and I'll need to do a repeat of briefing that agent.

CHAPTER 9

I inhale as I move out of bed. If I had been tempted to convince myself that last night had all been a dream that would have stopped at the twinge of well-used muscles. My wrists show bruises from the handcuffs. I run a finger over the abrasions and hiss at the sting. I drop my hands. Later. I'll think about how much I like the marks later.

My ringtone breaks the quiet of the room. Confused, I find my phone, conveniently plugged in, resting on the bedside table. Hope fills me just to desert me when I see Jeremiah's contact info. *Really Evie? You thought the Vigilante was going to call after last night?*

I need to focus. I'm not being totally ridiculous. The man who shared my bed had plugged in my phone before he snuck out. Next to my phone lays the medallion necklace the Vigilante had worn.

I analyze my ringing phone first. The surface has been wiped clean of fingerprints. I roll my eyes and answer the phone.

"Michaels."

"Evie? It's past eight, the medical examiner has started Officer James's autopsy. Where are you and Bradley?"

Shit.

"I'm sorry. I overslept. I don't think Agent Bradley is going to be able to drive me today. Can you come pick me up?"

The silence on the other end of the line makes me wince.

"What an asshole."

My laughter takes me by surprise. I love my partner.

"It's, uh, complicated."

"I'm sure it is. I'll be there at about thirty after. You owe me coffee."

I sigh. "I owe you, Jeremiah."

"Hey, don't mention it, kid. What are partners for?"

We say our goodbyes and hang up. I look at the medallion. I'm not a fan of religious items but I can't keep from picking it up after ensuring that this item, and probably every surface in the motel room, is free of fingerprints.

The metal of the medallion is stingingly cold, and I nearly drop it. Last night it had been warmed by the Vigilante's skin. Instead, I run my thumb over the image, feeling the bumps of the angel figure wielding a sword against the image of something with horns. The imagery is familiar but my non-caffeinated brain can't place it. A puzzle for a different time.

I hang the medallion between my breasts, not questioning the inclination. The medallion feels heavier than it looks.

I glance around the room again. The missing garbage making my lips purse. No coffee cups or the used condom to run DNA on. Smart. The Vigilante and I are on opposing sides, the sooner I remember that, the better.

One thing at a time, Evie.

There is a copycat to catch.

CHAPTER 10

Jeremiah

The outside of the motel appears grimier in the light of day. I hadn't looked at it when I left this morning, grabbing breakfast before getting to the ME's office. I pull into a parking spot with five minutes to spare and I get out to lean against the car. Evie and I will be driving enough today. I don't want to spend the next five minutes waiting in the car.

My partner will be out exactly when I told her to. She's always been painfully punctual. Goddamn Agent Bradley and whatever went down between them. Evie had sounded rough when I called her. My partner is the toughest nut around. If Bradley hurt her, I'll... have to figure out something to do. Evie wouldn't appreciate me threatening violence.

Violence hasn't done many good things for me in the past. I stare at my phone. Would my son pick up a phone call from me if he knew I'd turned over a new leaf? The alcoholism is still there, but my days of random bar fights and staying out all night to drown my sorrows are over. I started anger management classes at Evie's pushing. I even learned to meditate.

Peggy had good reason to leave me when she did. I wasn't a good role model to have around our son. My presence hurt people more than it helped and my ex-wife was a wise woman. She chose our son over trying to fix me, and I will never fault her for it.

That she passed away before I could pull my head out of my ass enough to apologize to her is a wound I carry on my soul. That I still haven't been able to apologize to Marcus is a wound that festers. The last time I'd seen him had been at Peg's funeral. I'd been drunk, and he'd been grieving. We traded angry words.

My finger hovers over his name in my contacts. He's never answered, but I need to try. Like Evie suggested, I don't know how Marcus is affected by my calls. There's a sliver of a chance he could pick up.

Today. Today is the day I'll try again. I don't think before I press the call button and put the phone next to my ear.

Each echoing ring hurts. The phone beeps. It's gone to voicemail. Again. I torture myself by hearing the sound of his voice. He sounds just like my brother when he talks. Freddy died overseas. Hearing Marcus sound so much like him is like a one-two punch to the throat.

"This is Detective Marcus White. Please leave me a message and I'll get back to—"

I end the call without leaving a message. He never calls back. I thought I could leave a message as I sometimes have. Be as brave as Evie's Gloria and speak into the void again on the small chance Marcus would hear me this time. I'm not that brave today.

The idea that Marcus would delete a message from me without hearing it viciously tears at me. It would be a

CHAPTER 10

confirmation of every terrible fear that resides in my mind that tells me it's too late to save our relationship.

Marcus told me he doesn't have a father. Maybe my real fear is that he'll pick up one day and tell me it wasn't anger talking.

I press the corner of the device into my forehead and take deep breaths, trying to loosen the tight knot in my chest. The grief of losing someone is a familiar companion to me. The grief of losing someone who is still around feels sharper somehow.

I swallow and slide my phone back in my pocket blindly.

A scrape of a boot too close startles me. Too late.

Pain blooms across my face as it collides with the car. My world spins and I'm so stunned I can barely fight the efficient tug on my holster. I reel as my gun skitters across the parking lot. Something hard is shoved against my head. *Gun barrel.*

A gasp has my assailant turning both of our bodies toward the motel. Files are scattered on the sidewalk, and Evie points a gun at us. I blink rapidly, trying to make the world stop tilting. She's pale.

"Drop the gun and kick it that way."

The perp yanks me bodily. His voice has a rasp and a detached tone. The grip he has on me is firm, he's similar to me in size, younger. His efficient movements from before have my heart sinking. I'd guess some sort of law enforcement or military.

"Let my partner go and we can start talking." Evie's voice doesn't shake. She is the picture of calm and collected, but I see the panic as her skin gets paler.

"Drop your gun and kick it away. There's no reason for your partner to die." There is an edge to the voice. No hesitation. He'll do it. The reason he hasn't is because there is something he wants more.

"Don't do it, Evie!"

Roaring despair fills me when she makes eye contact with me. Her eyes full of apology. She won't let me be killed for her own safety. She should, but she won't. Evie slowly lowers the gun to the concrete. The sound of it clattering away deafens me.

"Good. Now your cell phone."

I watch my partner sacrifice herself. Evie kicks the device away.

"Go over to the black car. The trunk is open."

Evie walks slowly over to the black sedan. It was there when I'd pulled in. I'd dismissed it when I saw it was empty. My distraction gave the unsub an opportunity. *My fault.*

When Evie gets to the trunk, there's a tremor in her hands. I tense to fight back, but the cold metal bites into my head harder. "Don't make me shoot you in front of your partner, Agent White."

"Please, Jeremiah," Evie says.

I stop struggling. The way Evie looks at me has me trying to take deep breaths. She's trusting me. If I struggle, he'll shoot me in the head. If I stay alive, I have a chance of being able to help Evie later.

"Take out the handcuffs and cuff yourself. Hands behind your back. Do it correctly."

It's difficult to get a read on the man's mental state. He is neither giddy nor snarling. The Copycat merely clearly states his orders and uses our titles. There is a tension to him, but without seeing his face I can't judge anything.

"Now, you're going to climb into the trunk, Agent Michaels."

CHAPTER 10

Evie's eyes are dark with fear.

The unsub starts to walk us slowly to the car. Sensing her hesitation. Evie doesn't like small dark places.

I breathe. I need to do something. Evie could mean to go through with it, but her hesitation could make the unsub impatient.

Now. I drop my bodyweight completely, but the man anticipates it. He sidesteps and throws me backward. There are two quiet pops and my body jerks as I fall to the asphalt. *Silencer.*

The wave of pain is blinding, and I'm only left with sounds as my body rebels. Evie's scream is cut off with a smack. A slam of a trunk and the revving of a car. She's gone.

I yell out nonsense, but it's useless. The motel parking lot is deserted. I prop myself up and see the blood. It doesn't look good. I try to master the pain to think. *Evie.*

I place one hand over where I'm bleeding and grit my teeth while I apply pressure. I have to stay conscious. My hand is slippery with blood, but I manage to take out my phone and dial dispatch. I give the codes needed.

"—I'm shot, but my partner was taken in a black sedan."

I don't have any details about the assailant. I never even saw the license plate. What I do know isn't enough to do more than put out a BOLO. *Evie is going to die.*

I give the address of the motel and the dispatcher says an ambulance is on the way and to stay on the line.

"Fuck that." I hang up.

I have to do something else. I have to help Evie. I've failed everyone who's ever relied on me. If I'm going to die, I won't have Evie's life on my soul too. My movements are already becoming slow. I have to hurry.

One unlikely option whispers its way under the pain and panic roaring in my chest. I dial a number that Evie isn't the only one to have memorized.

I try to focus while I hear the ringtone. I don't have much time left.

"Agent White?"

Of course, the fucker knows my number. No time. This gamble has to work.

"He has Evie. You have to help her. She's in the trunk of a black sedan. Left the motel within the last five minutes. I've been shot. I don't have any other details. I didn't know who else to call." I cough. My words are starting to slur. That's a bad sign. I take a leap of faith. "Tell her… tell her that I loved her like the daughter I never had."

"For fuck's sake Jeremiah, you can't die!" The man's voice sounds familiar. It ticks the possibilities that have been rolling around in my mind.

My laugh hurts. "That isn't for either of us to decide."

I hang up. One more call. I have to make one more call.

The phone rings.

It goes to voicemail again. This time I leave my message. Speaking into the void on the small chance it reaches him. It isn't bravery now, it's desperation.

"Marcus, I'm so sorry. For everything. For not being there. For not getting my shit together for you or your mother sooner. You're the best son a father could ask for. I'm so proud of you." My throat swells and I start to see spots in my vision. "I love you."

I hear sirens before the world goes dark.

CHAPTER 11

Evelyn

Pain splits through my head. I crack my eyes open and close them abruptly to focus on not vomiting. It's dark where I am. Dark and small. I breathe and wish away things slowly, deliberately. I wish away the nausea that climbs up my throat and the walls of wherever I am closing in on me. I wish that I hadn't been locked in places when I was a child, it still affects me.

I really wish the ground would stop shaking. *Trunk.*

Every so often the car must hit a pothole because it rattles my abused brain in my skull. My face feels wet. *Tears?* No. Places have dried and itch on my skin. I lick my lips and taste a metallic tang. *Blood.*

Things slide into place. The nausea is from a head wound. I was pistol-whipped and Jeremiah was—I try not to whimper. The Copycat has me. I'm in the trunk while we drive wherever the man wants to take me. *I'm in a trunk—stop it!* Being in a trunk is the least of my worries right now.

Jeremiah was shot. I saw blood. He isn't going to be able to come save me. If I'm really lucky, he's still able to notify the authorities to come after me, and for his own ambulance. I breathe. I can't worry about my partner right now.

If I have the luxury of a later, I'll worry about him later.

My arms ache where they are restrained behind me. I cuffed myself. First thing's first, I slide a pick from my watch and wish I had practiced this with my hands behind my back more. While my hands struggle, I analyze.

I was probably unconscious for less than five minutes. Most people lose consciousness for small amounts of time. Unless the Copycat drugged me. I don't think so. The man felt too much in a rush. Was taking me purely opportunistic?

The car hits a bump—hard. I try not to cry out as my head hits carpet again. The pick is knocked from my hand. Tears come to my eyes, but I focus and get another pick. This one isn't the best pick shape for this, but it will have to do. I start picking the handcuffs again. It's a simple lock, but my brain is dizzy, and my hands are sweaty.

Analyzing, I'm supposed to be analyzing. The Copycat has me. That is the most obvious answer. The escalation was expected. I had anticipated that Jeremiah and I working on this case would paint irresistible targets on us. Or me rather. The media enjoys crucifying me more than Jeremiah.

It's hard to remember details of the incident leading to this. I'd been walking out of the motel when I'd heard the sounds of a struggle. When I came upon them, my eyes had stayed glued to the gun digging into Jeremiah's skull.

I almost lose another pick from my fingers trembling. Somewhere in my brain, I dig up the sound of Malcom's voice as he'd guide me through a problem-solving exercise. *Focus, Evie, the gun is old news. What about the man?*

The man had been similar in build to Jeremiah, tall and broad. A blond buzz cut. Military? Law enforcement? The man had been quick, which indicated training. He had strength to make up for any training he lacked.

His appearance and bearing had been ordinary, but there had been a look in his eyes that struck a note of familiarity in me, my brain skips over that. The way he'd started directing the scene had been formal.

The handcuff pops. I sigh in relief and bring my arms in front, trying to massage out the stiffness.

His bearing had been unusual, intense, and concerned. What is his motive? The Vigilante targets individuals who escaped justice. The Copycat targets law enforcement. Where do the ideologies connect? Unless the Copycat just hates cops, a possibility, this line of thinking isn't going anywhere.

Approach this from another direction. I don't know how much more time I have until we get to our destination. Any insight could be helpful. That intensity he had... I've seen it before as a gleam in my grandfather's eyes when he spoke to a congregation.

Holy fire. That's what the older ladies in the congregation had called it. Righteousness that empowers individuals to do whatever they have to. The thought makes it hard to breathe.

The car stops.

Panic rises as I slide my hands over the rough carpeted interior of the trunk, checking for anything I can use. Normal trunks would have some light, but this trunk has been reinforced and I'm the only thing in it. That the trunk is reinforced already makes this crime more organized than any the Copycat has done so far.

I try to plan something as sounds reach me. The car door opening and slamming shut, then nothing for breaths until jangling. Chains being dragged on concrete. My stomach turns.

My holster is empty. I threw my gun away for Jeremiah. The only things on my person are my badge, ChapStick, saint medallion, and the key to my motel room. The first two items are useless, the third must be cursed, but the fourth item is better than nothing.

The motel is old school, no magnetic keycards, just an ugly brass room key with a number on it. Maybe it's old enough to have been used as a shiv before. If not, there's a first time for everything. No time to sharpen it into a better weapon.

I hear the footsteps approach and turn my body to face the trunk door. Keeping my hands behind my back as if I'm still restrained. I prepare myself for the struggle. I have to play the part until I see my opening. I'll only have one chance to use my chosen weapon.

He pops the trunk, and I kick out my legs at him. I hit the man, but he's so solidly built he barely staggers. The light is bright, and my aim isn't great. My head still swims from the impact of his gun earlier.

It's laughable how easily the Copycat handles me. He grabs me by my hair and pulls me from the car. It takes all my control to keep my hands from coming up to claw at the fist in my hair. This isn't the moment.

My feet hit the concrete and the pull on my hair lessens, but now the glint of a gun barrel is pointed at my face. I absorb information from our surroundings. We're in a warehouse. I can tell from the dusty light and the taste in the air.

The Copycat isn't even breathing hard. I thought my body had maxed out on fear, but I have to fight another wave of fright at the sight of the Copycat's serene face.

"Please don't struggle, Agent Michaels. I really don't want to have to hurt you, but I will if you make me." The Copycat speaks earnestly. The juxtaposition of those words with the proficient hold he has on my hair is chilling.

The Copycat's appearance is so at odds with my expectation. Calmness comes off the man. I wouldn't have looked twice if I passed him in the street.

"You don't want to hurt me? What about my partner? Your other victims? You've hurt lots of people." It's hard to keep my voice from shaking. The longer I can engage this man, the more opportunities I'll have. Opportunities to strike and for others to come to my rescue, if they're coming.

The Copycat's face winces in grief. I believe the emotion, but it's so inconsistent with the gun he has pointed in my face that my heart stutters.

"Causing pain has never been the plan. I would have left your partner alive if he had just done what I asked. The others didn't have to die painfully, but when they struggled it got messy. Why won't anyone listen? This task is already hard enough."

"Task?" Does he have someone he's working with? Receiving orders from? I try to steady my breathing. Had we missed something crucial?

The Copycat's face is solemn. "Duty. My calling. Please understand I don't want to do this, but it must be done."

Calling.

Chills run over my skin. "Why are you doing this? Who gave you this task?"

Wait for your moment, Evie.

The Copycat's smile is beatific. "When he opened the second seal, I heard the second living creature call out, 'Come!'—" The Copycat's voice is an eerie whisper.

My heart drops and acid stings my throat. I don't want to hear this, but he keeps on going.

"And out came another horse, bright red; its rider was permitted to take peace from the earth, so that people would slaughter one another; and he was given a great sword." He doesn't need to state what he's reciting. I shiver at the familiar intonation of scripture. *Revelations.*

"Would you like to take a moment to pray, Agent Michaels?"

I tremble. Dormant terror from my childhood has no place here, but that doesn't stop it from invading my senses, slowing my limbs and mind. The fervor of my grandfather still has the power to render me helpless.

I grip the key so hard it bites into my flesh. Trying to drive away the terror. I am not a helpless child being dragged to a dark closet with bruising force.

I nod, shaky. The Copycat relaxes at that. "Good. Take your time, Agent Michaels. Pour out your heart to your Creator."

A distant clanking sound has the Copycat looking away. Time slows in my mind. Now.

I strike. Trying to disarm the Copycat at the same time as aiming my key at his eyes.

My face hits concrete. The pain that had been a distant thing roars to the surface and I cry out. Everything had been a blur. I don't even have the motel key anymore. *I've failed.*

"I told you not to struggle." The Copycat's voice isn't angry, it just reverberates with disappointment.

Tears run down my face and a sob catches in my chest.

CHAPTER 11

The world turns again as the Copycat lifts me to my feet again but my legs buckle. So dizzy. My brain rebels from the abuse of being rattled yet again. I'd rather not vomit, but decide if I do, I'm aiming it at my enemy.

The man keeps me standing by his hand in my hair. The gun digging into my skull until I raise my hands in front of myself.

"If you don't choose to use this opportunity to pray, then we'll continue."

The Copycat walks me forward, the gun digs painfully. I stumble along, stiff and unfocused. The chain has already been strung around an upper walkway. In a removed way, I realize that my body will be left hanging in an artless way against a wall. It's insulting.

The Copycat keeps talking, each word getting more fervent. "I really wish you had prayed. I'd feel better about all of this if you made good with God. I'm sorry, Agent Michaels, but you are the enemy. Society will fall, but you're getting in the way of our Savior."

Rage sparks at this whole fucked-up situation. If this is where my life ends, it will not be steeped in fears and trauma that have persisted through all logic and reason. I can't let this happen.

I'll make him shoot me before I allow this zealot to hang me.

My muscles tense as I'm finally able to move past the ridiculous fears that plague me. A voice breaks through the warehouse air, strong and deep in the presence of the Copycat's demented whispers.

"Oh, you already started without me."

The Copycat swings us around toward the familiar voice, yanking my hair and pointing the gun toward our guest.

Gene stands there with his black-gloved hands raised. No panic in his face to having a gun pointed at him.

"You're that other FBI agent. H-how did you find us?"

That is a question we have in common. I soak in Gene's appearance. He is really here. I never expected to see him again.

My soaring hopes fall. The man in front of us isn't Agent Bradley, Gene, but a predator. This man, dressed in black with fathomless dark eyes, is the actualized form I'd only caught flashes of the night before. The Vigilante, the boogieman of criminals and haunter of my dreams.

The Copycat's calm breaks and his fist beginning to shake in my hair makes me wince.

The Vigilante raises his brows. "Are you sure about that? You think I wouldn't find my way onto the scene of someone who has taken up my teachings?"

Ignoring the question of how he found us, the crooning nature of the Vigilante's voice lulls my captor. My chest hollows, fear eating up my insides.

The Vigilante is an accomplished liar, that's a fact. But which is the lie? Last night or this moment? I can't tell, and I don't think the odds of him being here to help me are good.

"It-it's you! I didn't think we'd ever meet again!"

Confusion clouds my already foggy brain. The Vigilante's face is impassive, but his mouth curves.

"Fate must have had other plans."

"I knew it was you. I saw the news, all the reports, and I remembered the killing of that soldier all those years ago. It happened just like how those bodies were found. I was stationed near there. That Godless place, with soldiers doing Godless things. And then you struck! Like a miracle, the sinning stopped."

CHAPTER 11

The skin crinkles around the Vigilante's eyes, but I can't interpret the expression. Military. I'm annoyed with myself. There were no matching instances to these crimes in the systems I had access to. I should have dug into that avenue harder. The Copycat continues his fangirling. Each word makes me colder.

"I knew that when you started up that's how it would work! You'd punish the sinners. I finally knew my calling was to help you! Society has to fall for the second coming to happen."

The Vigilante barely glances at me. "That's why you went after the police officers. To usher in the fall of society?"

The Vigilante says this as if it's completely logical. As if he needs no further reason to string me up.

"The rider of the red horse. You understand!" Happiness buoys the Copycat's words.

"I understand. So, shall we do this?" The Vigilante smiles with all of his teeth and gestures to the dangling chain.

The Copycat shakes with excitement. "It would be an honor."

I'm pushed again toward the chain.

The bang deafens me, and my body is pulled down by my hair before I'm released. I turn to see the Copycat's body on the ground, a neat hole between his eyes and a mess behind his head.

My body starts to shake, violently. The Vigilante's eyes are on the Copycat. He almost looks sad. The gun still pointed at the fallen man.

A sob breaks from me, my sanity is dissolving into tiny pieces. The panic and fear don't leave me yet. The Vigilante finally turns to me and lets his mask fall. His face looks worried, he holsters his gun and takes a step toward me.

My hand comes to my mouth to stifle the next sob. I stumble back from him, but I'm too slow. His arms catch me and I'm sobbing into his body. Nothing makes sense.

"Evelyn... Evelyn. You need to breathe, Evelyn."

I can't breathe. I choke and try my hardest to keep from passing out in relief. Flashes of things happen. I can't track their order. *Shock, I'm going into shock.*

The Vigilante holding me in his arms. The Vigilante making me sit down a distance away from the body. The brush of lips on my forehead. The sound of sirens.

I'm alone with a body when the officers rush in.

CHAPTER 12

Evelyn

My thumb rubs over the saint medallion in a ritual. If I knew the rosary prayers, I wonder if I'd be tempted to pray. My knowledge of Catholicism is sparser than any desire I have to pray. So, instead, as I sit in the hospital waiting room, I feel metal beneath my thumb. Up the wings of whatever saint it depicts, over the sword, down the figure's body to the horned thing it fights against, and repeat.

Hours. I've been here for hours and the metal looks no different for all the times I've brushed it. Some part of me thinks if I can erode the image on the surface, I can erase what happened today. That the images of my time with the Copycat and Vigilante will disappear and Jeremiah will be healthy instead of being shot.

The medallion is the only method of distraction I have left. I can't work. I've been put on leave. Agents don't just get to turn up on the job again after getting abducted. Mountains of paperwork and psych evaluations will have to be scaled before I'm allowed to return to work. That's before I confess to calling the Vigilante. If they ever read that report. The future in front of me is riddled with winding paths that lead to unknown places.

I already gave my statement. That had certainly left the officials scratching their heads. *A good Samaritan showed up and shot the assailant?* I just shrugged in response. The whole scenario was labeled bizarre, and that was the end of it.

He saved my life. The man who committed horrific crimes and I am the one responsible for bringing him in... but he saved me from being the next person hanging from a chain. A life debt.

I've been told I should be resting in a hospital bed of my own. I have a concussion. I let the medical professionals check me out, but I can't rest. Not when Jeremiah is under the knife.

I keep vigil for my best friend. Me and this suspicious medallion, waiting in this waiting room.

A man comes into the room. His stature is familiar. Broad shoulders and tall but closer to me in age. He sees me and starts in my direction. Annoyance brews in me but I tamp it down.

Maybe one good thing can come from all of this. If Jeremiah wakes up that is.

The man vibrates with emotion and my body feels even more tired. I should stand and shake his hand, but everything hurts right now. I forgive myself for not making the effort to get to my feet when the man starts to speak to me.

"You're Evelyn Michaels." A statement, not a question.

"Yes, and you're Marcus White."

He starts as if I've surprised him.

"You look just like your father," I say.

Something ugly passes over Marcus's face. Maybe if my skull wasn't pounding, I would be able to interpret the undercurrent of this conversation.

CHAPTER 12

"How is he?"

"Sit, please." I gesture to the seat across from me, but Marcus doesn't move. I sigh. "I'm concussed, I won't talk to you if I have to look up to do it, and I'm not standing before I have to."

Marcus relents and sits mechanically. A promising start. Not.

"As you are already informed, I'm Evelyn Michaels, Jeremiah's partner."

There is a scoff at that that has my brows raising but I continue, "Jeremiah was shot twice today. One bullet was stopped by his bulletproof vest, but the other got him just under it. He's been in surgery for a long time."

I rub the medallion again to ground myself. "The doctor said that they will tell me as soon as they have news. Jeremiah and I arranged to have medical power of attorney for each other in case of situations like this." *In case no one else showed up.*

If anything, the look on Marcus's face turns darker.

My protective instinct rises at his reaction. "If you're here to pick a fight with your father, or cause him any distress, I'm going to ask you, politely, to leave. I will inform you of the prognosis either way."

I choke on those last words.

"And I should just trust whatever you tell me?"

"You could have picked up any of the calls from Jeremiah if you didn't want an intermediary." My jaw is tense. I shouldn't rile up Jeremiah's son, but this distraction is a breath of fresh air. "You don't even know me."

"Evelyn Michaels, daughter of a single mother who died when you were ten. Leaving you to be raised by your grandfather, Jackson Michaels. He seems like a fun person to be around; I saw his sermon about AIDS being the cure for homosexuality distributed by his church years ago. Moved into the home of Malcom Bates and his wife at age sixteen and was recruited by the FBI straight out of college."

Silence falls and I stare at Marcus, confused. He knows my background. Why did he bother looking me up?

"Did I miss anything?" Marcus asks.

"Lots. Like, why you seem to hate me."

"Why would I like a woman younger than me sleeping with my father?"

I'm stunned. Then I do something very unwise for someone with a concussion. I start laughing. My laughter is short-lived because, *fuck*, it's painful.

I wipe away tears of mirth and pain, and Marcus suddenly doesn't look as sure as he had been before snarling at me.

"I know about you too, you know. Marcus White, the Hero Detective, broke all the rules to save the last victim of that serial killer in your city. Jeremiah wouldn't stop talking about it for weeks. He was very proud." I have to stop at the thought of how cheerful Jeremiah had been.

Marcus looks surprised, his cheeks pinken charmingly. I continue, "Jeremiah is my best friend. We have never, will never, be together romantically."

I close my eyes, letting my head rest on my hands. I'm not in a great condition to verbally spar with the Hero Detective, a much better moniker than Ice Queen in my humble opinion, so I let the conversation lapse into silence. Blessed uneventful minutes go by but now I'm back to worrying about Jeremiah.

Marcus clears his throat awkwardly and I open my eyes.

"I owe you an apology," he says.

"You think so? That was quick."

"Dad has been leaving messages on my phone—"

"Because you won't answer."

Marcus nods. "Because I haven't been answering. Just some passing comments he made about his partner 'Evie' had me thinking you guys were close."

"We are close. Just not in the biblical way. Anyway, someday your father might meet someone. I should hope that you treat them better than you've treated me."

Marcus looks away, his eyes are red-rimmed and my hope that this does resolve in a way that makes Jeremiah happy climbs. Marcus wears shame like a heavy cloak. *How much had his disgust of me been propping the man up?*

"It's not that I don't want him to find anyone else. I think. It was just your age… *fuck*, I don't know." Marcus lets out a shuddering sigh.

"I predict there are so many issues between your father that liking who he dates should take a back seat. It's okay to be worried about him. I'm terrified."

Marcus looks at me in surprise. "You don't look terrified."

My patience with the man in front of me is sand reaching the end of an hourglass. "Because you always wear your emotions on your sleeve? Don't insult my feelings for Jeremiah because I'm not wailing in the hallways. I had hoped you were a better detective than you were a son, but so far all of your assumptions have been poorly made and unsubstantiated."

Marcus looks like I've slapped him, and I take one moment of satisfaction before regret seeps in. I don't want Marcus to leave without Jeremiah having a chance to talk to him. Then again, if I can chase Marcus off with a few sharp words, maybe it's better he leave now.

"You're right. I-I'm fucking this up." Marcus's voice is tight and he drops his head in his hands, fingers winding through his hair in frustration. "Can I apologize again?"

I cough and laugh at the same time. Ridiculous man.

"Maybe we can just sit in silence and try not to piss each other off."

Marcus sighs. "If we aren't arguing, I'll have nothing to do but remember all the phone calls I've screened from Dad and the last phone message he sent me." It comes out quiet.

I ache a little. If I had been fighting with Malcom before he died, I'd be a wreck. But I'm not the one he should be asking for forgiveness. I try to make my voice gentle. "Yours is an earned pain. I think sitting and contemplating your wrongdoings isn't the worst thing you could do."

Marcus's laugh is harsh and pained. The tension between us melts. "Jesus Christ, you're a tough judge. If I didn't know you grew up with evangelicals, I'd think you were Catholic. Did you convert or something?"

Marcus gestures toward the medallion I'm holding, and I smile at that.

"No, God doesn't want me. This was a… gift. I don't even know what saint is on it."

Marcus reaches out his hand to see, and I have to force myself to hand over the artifact. I'm too attached to the charm. But I succeed in giving it to him.

The medallion is tiny in Marcus's hands and the man considers the design.

"It's an apt gift. St. Michael, patron saint of police officers, slaying the devil."

That sonofabitch.

Marcus continues with a frown, "It's thicker than any medallion I've seen."

I already noted that and have some suspicions. I hold out my hand and want to scold myself for how relieved I am when Marcus gives it back to me. The metal is still warm from both of our hands. I should throw the medallion away, but I can't make myself do it.

"Evie."

Marcus and I look up at the voice. *Oh shit.*

Gloria stands there, creased navy pantsuit and blonde bob frizzy. She looks like an angel to me. An angel with a tear-stained face. "I heard you were abducted. On the news, Evie. I heard you almost died from a newscaster. I can understand you ignoring my phone calls. Everyone grieves differently. But you didn't call to tell me you were okay?"

Shame sickens me. Marcus clears his throat.

"Hmm. Ignoring phone calls? 'He that is without sin among you, let him first cast a stone'… or something like that." Marcus is lighter when he stands, almost cheerful. As if seeing my own sins thrown back at me gives us a comradery. Maybe it does. "I'm going to the cafeteria to get coffee. Either of you want any?"

I burn. Marcus is right. I'm a hypocrite. My chest is so tight that my breath is trapped, I can't speak. Gloria gives a polite 'no thank you.' Marcus's footsteps echo as he leaves me with the woman I respect so greatly that I couldn't manage to answer any of her damn calls.

I don't want her to know how far I've fallen.

"Do you want me to leave?" Gloria's trembling voice breaks my stupor.

"No! I'm sorry, you just surprised me. I've… I've had a bad day." To my horror, my eyes begin to fill with tears and my throat swells.

Gloria opens her arms and my heart moves me into them. A homecoming. The embrace makes my body shake and my tears stream down my face. Gloria cradles me. Ever since I moved in with her and Malcom, she's claimed me as hers. Pushed me to get counseling when Malcom felt too uncomfortable about the topic to try. She and Malcom never had kids of their own, but she once told me, *When people ask me about my children, I tell them about my beautiful, courageous daughter.*

"I'm so sorry, Gloria. I just… I couldn't…" My voice breaks.

Gloria makes shushing sounds in my hair. "It's okay. You're okay."

I'm not. I'm not okay, but I let myself be lulled by her words, her warmth.

"I've been stupid," I whisper.

"I doubt that."

I've driven my mental and physical state into the ground trying to avoid the drowning grief I feel when I think about Malcom being gone forever. I *fucked* a serial killer.

"You don't even know what I've done."

"I still doubt it." The trust this woman has in me is a gift. I give myself this moment of being in her arms. It's a balm for my ragged emotions.

Gloria pulls away first. "I think you need someone to talk to. Let's sit and you can fill me in."

"There's too much—" I make a gesture up to my own head as if in explanation while we sit side by side. It's easier when I'm not facing her. "If I start talking, I don't know where I'll stop."

I don't want to divulge the extent of my actions. To rain down a confession of my misdeeds to this woman. I don't want to come to terms with the fact that out of all the things I've done, I don't regret my actions with the Vigilante.

Gloria's hands come up and cradle my face, turning me to look at her.

"I understand that we're waiting for your partner to come out of surgery. I'd say we have the time for you to hash this out."

I hesitate. Am I ashamed or guilty? I can't tell.

"Have you hurt innocents?" she asks. Does Jeremiah count? No, he signed up for this job, and as low as my feelings are right now, him getting shot wasn't my fault.

I shake my head.

"My love for you is unconditional. I'll be honest, Evie, you're the last thing I have left of my life with Malcom. It might not be morally right for me to always be on your side, but you are my family. If I'm still yours, that is."

"Of course you're still my family! Gloria, I just—" I shake my head. "I feel so fucking guilty. For everything. For freezing you out. For never visiting when Malcom was alive. And just for the mess I've made of everything…" Sins upon sins rain down on me. Each is a small cut contributing to a widening pain.

Gloria's lips purse on her no-nonsense face. "All that guilt has done for me is make me feel like I've lost you. Let it go, Evie. It's time you stop hiding."

Her matter-of-fact tone has a small smile stealing its way onto my face. This woman has always known what to say to me.

I bury my pride and ask for help. I tell Gloria everything.

The conversation is over long before the doctor comes out with news about the surgery.

Part 2: Absolution

CHAPTER 13

Eugene

The burn is excruciating. The barbell shakes in my grip, but with a grunt, I keep it from crushing me and hook it into the rack. I lay on the weight bench letting my muscles seize. Pain is the most direct way to harness my focus.

I sit up and my muscles scream at me; I relish it. Before the weight bench, I'd run as much as my leg could handle. My limp is almost more pronounced now than a month out after surgery. Multiple times I've worked myself to exhaustion, sought the clearness that pain provides.

It's not working.

It's been one month since I'd snuck my way into an FBI investigation. One month since meeting the esteemed Special Agent Evelyn Michaels in person rather than just viewing her face on the television or hearing her voice over the phone. One month since abandoning her in a warehouse next to the body of my most recent victim.

The last moment I saw her is burned into my bones, a mere muscle ache can't compete.

I'm a fucking mess.

I've been a mess for years but this is different. This has affected my mission. I missed the date of the last planned execution. A week after the Copycat case had been what the world expected of me, and I missed it. I don't have my head in the game. Three weeks later and I still can't make myself focus.

Instead of taking out my planned target, I released an info packet to the media. Maybe this man, who had his wife killed so he could avoid a messy divorce, will be able to be dealt with through traditional means. Maybe I don't have to be the one to bring him to justice.

I may not have my head together enough to physically take out the guilty, but I can't just let him go either. The media is going nuts that my spree has been broken. How had Evelyn taken the info packet without the murder?

Every time I close my eyes, memories haunt me. Her icy glare, the sounds I'd coaxed to spill from her mouth, haughty and precise even when handcuffed. The unbelievable heat of her body around mine.

Focus, Eugene!

I let out an exasperated sigh and rise from the weight bench. One night with the woman has destroyed my equilibrium. Sleep isn't an option, work just ends with me staring into space.

The alternative memories aren't helpful either. Those wait in the dark recesses of my mind. The memory of Officer Miller's body hanging. The sounds of his crying wife in the background of Jeremiah's phone call. The pure joy on the Copycat's face.

Evelyn isn't the only reason I've hesitated.

The Copycat, Jacob Trier, had been inspired by my actions. The actions I took in the very beginning. The guilt is a discomfort that wraps around me like barbed wire. Could more individuals be influenced into violence from my work? How culpable am I in crimes someone else commits?

I sit down at the desk of my home office and take a moment to look at the framed photo beside my computer. It's always served as an altar of sorts. A direction when everything else is so loud. Every time I come home from a killing, weary and sick, I'd take in the happy face of the blonde woman and let my rage realign me.

The photo doesn't punch me in the soul the way it used to. As if the infection has finally leaked from the wound. Except, I still want to hurt. I want to press on the bruise of losing Kaitlyn because how else can I make myself string up the guilty? How else can I risk instigating more Jacob Triers? *An uprising of vigilantes.*

I sigh.

With time and distance, my past has become less of a throbbing wound and more of a cliché story.

Does a certain FBI agent add deviation to this story?

Before I'd seen Special Agent Evelyn Michaels make a televised announcement in one of the early cases, I would have laughed myself silly at the suggestions that my crimes had a sexual component. But seeing *her* in front of the flashing lights, outlining the crime I'd committed, shifted something. Her attention is intoxicating.

Evelyn… for months I've watched her through the media coverage of the Vigilante case. The agent with the cutting eyes and severe personality stole my sanity. Her name is the perfect coincidence. The saint, pure perfection. It makes me want to dirty her. Tarnish those cold eyes and perfect actions, to show I had been there. A perverse hunger locked away in my soul.

Agent Michaels, from a distance, gleams with perfection; a paragon of virtue. Untouchable by the likes

CHAPTER 13

of me. Then she called me, had ignored the rules, and that changed everything. Anyone would have given into the temptation of seeing a saint on earth; but to be an instrument in corruption? ... The potency of the idea was too heady to ignore.

I hadn't meant for everything to happen that did. I had only meant to get information about the Copycat, meet her, the woman who kept me up at night. Taste the air around her. *Fuck* I don't know. I've never been drawn to anyone like I am to her.

I had expected to meet the saint. Instead, the first meeting of Special Agent Evelyn Michaels had been her in a blonde wig, dropping to her knees in front of me, and swallowing my cock down her throat.

Under conventional thinking, the action should have destroyed the image of her perfection. It hadn't. It had made her real. The bruises under her eyes from lack of sleep, the wildness barely contained within her skin. Her steel spine and steelier words. The exposed vulnerability under Evelyn's competence makes me ache. My want for her is a visceral thing.

Thinking of Evelyn has me hard without a second breath. I glare across the room at the weight bench. My unruly body always responds to the memories no matter how far I push it. Exercise and pain can only provide so much of a distraction. Jacking off just enhances the hunger I feel for her.

Meeting Evelyn was supposed to satisfy my curiosity, not escalate my obsession. There has been no media coverage since the Copycat case except that Agent Jeremiah White had survived his injury. That had been a relief, but I itch to see the woman who destroyed all of my good sense in less than a day.

Across from the framed photograph of Kaitlyn is a pinned photo. The photo is pinned facing the wall. I had come home from the Copycat case, seen Evelyn's eyes looking at me from that photo, and had known I needed to distance myself. The action of turning the photo had been purposeful. Out of sight, out of mind. It hasn't worked.

My purpose has been shattered with the memory of Evelyn's face, pale with terror and smeared with vivid blood. Anger brews. One woman will not be the reason my mission fails.

Even if one woman was the reason behind the mission?

I should just rip off the Band-Aid. Give into the curiosity, see what the FBI has been up to. Seeing their efforts to track me down will undoubtedly refocus me. My angel is more equipped than ever to find my identity, knowing that she's after me should spur me back into action.

Special Agent Michaels, not my angel, not my anything.

My real job is in cyber security. I have the skills for the work, and it provides flexibility for my extracurricular activities. When the FBI got involved with the Vigilante case, I made sure I'd be able to get the inside scoop. I scan through the memos and emails being sent back and forth, but there is a name missing from all the usual documents.

Evelyn isn't listed on any of the current documents detailing that no headway has been made in identifying the Vigilante. Jeremiah's name is also missing, but there is an older document announcing his retirement.

My breath freezes in my chest. Is she okay? If the revelations during our night together are to be believed, they wouldn't remove her from the unpopular job of apprehending me. Would she ask to be transferred? It doesn't seem like her to just let the case go for no reason.

Could she be on a mental health leave? She had appeared shaken after the violence of her abduction. Her skin had been so pale, the freckles on her cheeks had been visible. I'd missed the marks in the dark of the night before.

What if all of these weeks that I've been trying to forget her, she has needed help? Someone to make her feel safe.

Do not be ridiculous, Eugene. If she needs someone to help her feel safe, that person isn't you.

I shake myself from that line of thinking. After everything I've done, I can't be a person who could be there for Evelyn. Even if I wanted to.

Do I want to?

It doesn't matter. What matters is finding Evelyn.

I let myself do something that I'd restrained myself from doing. I bring up the tracking software on the medallion.

The medallion had been mine. It had started as testing new technology with a company I do work for every so often. But after a few weeks of wearing it, seeing it track my every movement, I discovered something. Some odd compulsion in me liked having a record.

It shouldn't have been so surprising that pulling up my location history after a mission satisfied me. It was my own method of reliving the hunt. It further demonstrated that I'm no different than any other serial killer. Knowing all of this, I kept the medallion.

A split-second decision of leaving it in the motel room, leaving it for the object of my unhealthy obsession, saved Evelyn's life.

It had been a near thing. The world had been very close to no longer having Evelyn Michaels in it. The thought still has the power to leave me as cold inside as a glass pane in winter.

I would have never gotten there in time if she hadn't been wearing that medallion.

That she still wears it, that it still functions, is a long shot. My angel is a smart cookie, she would have figured out how I got there that morning just in time to stop Trier from making her his fourth victim.

What would it mean if she still wore the tainted piece of jewelry? Would it mean that she wanted me to find her? The answer to those questions doesn't matter. The tracker in the medallion is probably dead. Even so, I pull up the software and huff out a breath.

My disappointment is sharp.

The tracker isn't functioning. The last ping had been in the vicinity of the hospital Jeremiah had been at a little less than three weeks after the abduction. That she had kept it on her for that long is a curious detail. I won't be able to use that method to track her down. That leaves my usual methods.

I dig. It takes hours but each snippet of info I retrieve acts as a compulsion to find more.

Special Agent Evelyn Michaels is officially off the Vigilante case. There are some useless emails thanking her for the work she'd done but nothing else. It appears as if she left the FBI but there were no formal going away parties. Some of her coworkers have an email chain full of speculation about the "extended" leave of Agent Michaels. More than a few implied that she is getting comfy at a mental institution.

CHAPTER 13

The thought of the bright and beautiful Evelyn being institutionalized restricts my lungs. Each gasping breath causing pain.

Evelyn has never been my enemy. She's always been a danger to my mission, to me. But Evelyn, as a person, isn't my enemy. Her presence in the world gave me hope. *An avenging angel.*

I've always kept information that would be considered borderline, some not so borderline, stalking. None of the information is helpful.

I keep digging. The lease Evelyn had with her roommate has been altered, listing a new tenant who already moved in. The car she had has been sold. She's gone.

One avenue tempts me. It will be the quickest way to get the information I need. It's more risk than I should imbibe in, but desperation claws my heart. I'm having more feelings than is appropriate about this.

I pull up the number I'm looking for and dial it with a burner phone from my desk using a spoofing method to cloak the number on the receiving end to show a number from Virginia.

"Hello?" The woman on the phone sounds confused.

I read the time, calculate the difference, and realize it's ten p.m. where she is. I want to curse.

"Hello, is this Gloria Bates?"

I slip into a persona, modulating my voice just so to fit the nuance of a telemarketer. There's an ease that comes from the act. This kind of deception is one that I've come to excel at. It's a thrill all its own to assume an identity like this. A telemarketer alias pales in comparison to acting the part of Agent Bradley right under Evelyn's watch, but this action is comforting in its familiarity.

I lean back in my chair, tilting to balance on the back legs. I'll determine that Evelyn is alright and then I'll be free to devote myself to the mission.

"It is." Gloria sounds as if she's a hair away from hanging up.

I lower my voice, injecting seriousness into my tone. I need to keep the woman on the phone.

"You're listed as the emergency contact for an Agent Evelyn Michaels—"

"Oh my god! Did something happen?"

I hadn't meant to cause the woman to panic. The chair legs creak. I continue, trying to pacify the woman. "Now Mrs. Bates—"

"Is it the baby?"

Suddenly I'm weightless before I drop. My heart drops, my mind drops, my body drops. The impact of me clattering to the floor is white noise. The phone skitters away.

Baby?

There's no air, I gasp, stunned. I can't breathe. My mind starts to catch up as I'm finally able to breathe in. I scramble for the phone.

"Sorry, wrong number."

I hang up. Thoughts whir too fast for me to catch. I right myself and the chair, moving slowly. If Evelyn is pregnant… if she's carrying my—

I stop myself. What has really changed? I'm still a criminal. I've still killed people. I don't have anything to offer the world, but the violence delivered by my blood-soaked hands.

Still.

I reach for the pinned photo with precise motions and unpin it from the wall. Turning the photo in my hands

CHAPTER 13

until Evelyn's cold eyes are spearing me from the glossy photo.

I need a plan.

CHAPTER 14

Eugene

The cabin-like house is idyllic, set serenely in a heavily wooded forest. A forest where it will snow soon, maybe in a few weeks. The air is crisp and burns with fall flavors. It should make me shiver but I'm too on edge for that.

Quick items flick through my mind at the logistics of location. The driveway is paved at least and there is a healthy woodpile on the side of the house. Did Evelyn chop the wood herself? Or maybe a nice guy from the little town I'd just driven through had done it for her. My fists clench in my coat pockets.

Stop it, Eugene.

Evelyn is beautiful, single, and living in the middle of nowhere. The men in that tiny town are probably climbing over each other to get her attention. Maybe she even welcomes it. I had been the one to leave her high and dry. I had reasons… What if she is already someone else's angel?

No "what-ifs." The what-ifs won't stop this confrontation from happening and I wouldn't want them to.

All that matters is that Evelyn is here. I had to track her down through her finances. It had been a whole process. The "Where in the world is Evelyn Michaels" game and tying up loose ends in my life had taken another month on top of the one I had already spent without her.

But now I'm here, and it's more difficult than I thought it would be to take the steps required to bring me to her door. Everything is conjecture right now. Did she want me to find her? Did she move on with another man? *Is she pregnant?*

The sooner I walk up to the lovely cabin and knock on the door, the sooner I'd know what the fuck I am going to do. Either I'll have a future to figure out whether any of my conjectures are true or she'll shoot me on sight. That's a cheerful thought.

My legs move. Too soon, I'm up the porch and raising my hand to knock.

"What are you doing here?" The voice comes from behind me, as crisp and steely as anytime I've ever heard her.

Slowly I turn, raising both hands. An inherent instinct tells me that Evelyn wouldn't have snuck up and gotten the drop on me without a purpose. As much as I wished differently, we aren't on friendly terms. Yet.

Sure enough, Evelyn stands on the path I'd just walked, aiming a shotgun aptly at my heart. Her stance isn't a fearful one, she doesn't cower. Instead, Evelyn has an air of annoyance and suspicion, holding the firearm in a casual grip. As if we had run into each other at the grocery store and she'd rather not stop and talk to me. Not as if a serial killer had been about to knock on her door.

Fearless woman.

How long has she known I was here? I'd been standing motionless at the head of the driveway for an embarrassing amount of time.

"You didn't think I'd come?" I try to make my heartbeat slow. Being held at gunpoint isn't a relaxing experience, even if the gun is being held by the woman that has made my chest ache every day I'd spent away from her, especially then. I don't want adrenaline to make my decisions for me. Either Evelyn hates me enough to shoot me now or she wants me on edge for this discussion and the name of this trip is Lady's Choice.

Evelyn cocks an eyebrow. "Why would you? There didn't seem to be anything you wanted to hang around for last time. You left."

I try not to wince. Evelyn's poker face is solid, but I assume she is hurt by the way we parted.

"I had to go. You would have arrested me. You know you would have."

"And I won't arrest you right now? Knowing who you are?"

I step forward, closing some of the distance. *How stupid am I that I'm daring a federal agent to shoot me?*

Evelyn's face looks exasperated and answers my inner musings. *Very.*

"I hope not." This is my time to make my case and my mind stumbles. Is it the presence of the gun or the woman in front of me? She looks different. I've only seen her in business apparel, or out of it; the flannel and jeans she wears now makes her looks soft and approachable in comparison. Her face is still all delicate coldness, a sharpness ready to cut. Tear my heart to shreds.

"What are you hoping for, Gene? I hear nothing from you for months and you show up."

"You know I called Gloria," I state.

Evelyn raises her brows.

"You know what she told me…" I hesitate to continue.

CHAPTER 14

Her eyes shutter. Whatever emotions she's experiencing, I'm not privy to them. "There isn't anything here for you, Gene. Or whatever your name is."

Does she mean... I don't know what she means. Everything about this moment is precarious. As if we stand on glass that will shatter as soon as I ask if she's pregnant. If the glass shatters, I can't look at her anymore. Things will be pushed into motion and I won't be able to analyze the ways she's changed in the last couple months.

Evelyn is still as achingly beautiful as when I left her blood-smeared, but she looks tired and has lost weight she can't afford to lose.

The setting sun gleams off her dark hair, fiery copper highlights that my fingers itch to touch. Of course she arranged for my position to be facing the sun. She'd take any advantage possible.

Any. Advantage.

The pregnancy could have been a setup. I'd known that was a possibility even as I closed out the lease on my apartment, even when I burned my files. It could have even been real and now be over, whether by miscarriage or abortion.

I'm not going to ask. I want to know but it doesn't make a difference to my goal.

"It's Eugene. I like it when you call me Gene."

She narrows her eyes when I don't voice the question she expects. Her next words come out as a whisper. "Why are you here, Gene?"

"For you. I'm here for you."

"To tie up loose ends?"

I scoff at that. "If you really thought that, you would have shot me by now."

"I don't believe you."

I nod. I hadn't expected her to fall down in joy over the prodigal lover's return. There is a small stab of pain in me, but I deserve her distrust.

"Then I'll stay until you do believe me."

Evelyn

Surprise has me blinking. "What?"

Gene's eyes are achingly serious. "You don't trust me. You have your reasons. I admit they're good reasons. So, I'm staying until you do believe me."

This fucking guy.

I have a gun aimed at him and he tells me he's staying. "And just where are you staying?"

The humor glinting in Gene's dark eyes tells me I hadn't disguised my irritation nearly as well as I wanted to.

"In my car to start. I did see a motel on my way here. I have good memories involving motels." *Teasing.* This man is teasing me. I'd known since he called Gloria that he'd find a way to find me and had anticipated many outcomes to this scenario, but this hadn't been one.

Why hasn't he asked?

Since he hasn't asked, I can't make any of my pre-planned arguments. I can't accuse him of only being here because of that, and I can't tell any of the lies I had planned to. Gene's dark form had shown up in my life again and already toppled more than a few well-laid plans.

I skip ahead in my arguments and just go to the conclusion. "I don't want you here."

Gene winces and guilt eats at me. As much as I wish it, I'm not heartless toward this man. For weeks I've waited to see him again, sure that I would, and tried to convince myself it's because I wanted to get this over with. Not because the idea of seeing him makes my heart race. Not because I still dream of the night we spent together.

Gene takes a step forward while I wallow in guilt. He still moves like a predator, like he did that morning with the Copycat. This Gene holds only the smallest similarity to the Agent Bradley role he played. It doesn't help me that I prefer this version of him. My body is on alert, still hungry for the dangerous boogeyman.

Gene checks to see if my finger is on the trigger before he takes another step. Good to know he isn't suicidal, even as the barrel of the shotgun presses against his chest.

"Give me a chance to change your mind." The soft way he speaks strokes over my senses. A sensual quiver works its way up my spine.

I will not let this man seduce me. Again. There is more than my future at stake.

"Gene, there isn't anything for you here." I wish I wasn't breathless. I wish I sounded surer instead of like a broken record.

The man tilts his head. "You're here."

I'm not for you.

I can't say it. I need to say it. I might even want to say it, but I can't. I bite my lip, struggling with the proximity. Struggling to make good choices.

His hand comes up; maybe to cradle my face. Why am I letting him this close to me? Instead of touching my face, a tickle at my neck makes me shiver. The sound of metal on metal snaps me out of the sensual ease and I burn with embarrassment.

Gene pulls the medallion from under my shirt. He makes a sigh of satisfaction, as if he's received some answer that he had been looking for. Our eyes meet and his brim with heat. A purpose burns through him and the fire of it spreads to me.

A voice shatters the moment.

"Eugene, is it? Or are you going by something different now? Evie, you might want to put down the gun unless you are going to shoot him."

CHAPTER 15

Evelyn

I jump, raising the gun and spin toward Gloria's smiling countenance. Jeremiah is there with her, biting his stoic lips as if he's going to laugh at me. I must be slipping if I missed their approach.

They're carrying grocery bags and probably walked from the cabin Jeremiah moved into down the road. Jeremiah is holding Gloria's hand. I give him a look and lift a brow at their clasped hands. Jeremiah gives me a look and casts his eyes to Gene.

Well, he's right there. I can't judge him when I've been caught with this man.

"It's Eugene. Eugene Peterson," Gene answers Gloria. Surprise arches his eyebrows, but his quick mind takes in the couple's presence, probably deducing the details. So adaptive.

Did he just give a real name?

"He was just leaving," I say.

"I was?"

I clench my jaw and his eyes brighten in delight, but he puts his hands up. "I was just leaving. It's good to see you healthy, Agent White. And you must be Gloria Bates. We spoke on the phone."

Gene offers a hand to Gloria and she shakes it, a small smile on her lips. "Maybe we'll be seeing more of you soon, Eugene."

"I'll walk you to your car. It's the completely nondescript rental on the road, isn't it?" Jeremiah says, his smile tight.

I can't read Gene's facial expression, it lies somewhere between a grimace and a smile, but he nods.

I freeze. "Jeremiah—"

"Come on, dear. Help me with the groceries and let Jeremiah have his heart-to-heart," Gloria whispers.

"Heart-to-heart?" But I follow Gloria into the cabin. This whole situation has tumbled out of my control and I need to regroup.

Gene's comment about seeing Jeremiah healthy delivers a punch to my chest.

The antiseptic smell is mild, but it sears each moment I'm in this hospital into my memory. It's a collection of memories now. Getting butterfly bandaged and scanned while still shaking from the aftereffects of the abduction. The painful talk with Gloria. The interminable terrible waiting.

If I go years before going back to a hospital, it will be too soon. But it's not going to be years, not with what I just confirmed. I breathe out shakily.

"Are you going to tell me what you came here to tell me? Or are we just going to sit here in silence?" Jeremiah rests his head back. His hospital bed is elevated.

He looks better every day, but seeing him laid up still jars me. At least his skin has lost the gray hue that had clung to it after the surgery. Jeremiah had always been the definition of strength and support. But in a hospital gown, gray whiskers,

CHAPTER 15

and supported by pillows, the possibility of death feels too close. Jeremiah almost hadn't made it.

I try not to let myself go down that thought process. Most of the time, when he's not right in front of me, I can avoid the terror of him dying. My visitor's chair is angled so we don't need to stare at each other straight on. I close my eyes and try to keep my voice from wobbling.

"So, you and Marcus sorted things out?"

I'd watch their apologies happen at a distance. It had been weeks of the men hemming and hawing about every topic under the sun until they had both broken down.

"We've started to. I told him I'm going back to AA. That I've been going to counseling, trying to put the 'functioning' back in functioning alcoholic."

"He went back to work?"

"My health is getting better all the time. Even if you can't bear to look at me."

That hurts. It should hurt.

"I'm sorry, some fucking partner I am. It's just… it's hard seeing you like this."

Jeremiah hums. "Probably just as hard as it is for me to see you, day in and day out, with shadows in your eyes."

I make myself look at him. His eyes are soft, gentler than at any part of our partnership. Uncomfortable emotions well. He's my best friend and I almost lost him. My mind tries to find something else to think about, it finds it.

I frown. "You shaved?"

Jeremiah's cheeks pinken. The reaction is so curious that it takes me a moment to puzzle together the reason.

"You old dog."

Gloria should be around soon. She's been visiting Jeremiah with me the whole time.

"We aren't talking about me right now. We are talking about why you look like you're off to face the executioner."

Fuck.

I look away. "I'm resigning. The Bureau, it's just not the place for me. It fosters unhealthy behaviors for me. The work environment…"

Jeremiah just nods. "They never deserved you."

He sounds unsurprised.

"I think I'm going to go into consulting. It's more… flexible."

Why is it so hard to talk about this?

"You'll do well, going into business for yourself. I assume you have some starting capital."

"Malcom left me some funds."

"Have you decided where you'll set up base? I don't expect you'll move back to your hometown."

I shudder. That would be awful.

"I'm not exactly sure yet. Maybe somewhere more remote. An internet connection and nearby airport should be all I need. Gloria wants to live somewhere with mountains. Maybe a cabin."

"Mountains sound nice. I'm sure we can find a couple cabins. Not anywhere that gets too cold. You have older folks to think about."

My brain snags. "Excuse me?"

"Oh, you thought you were going to go do all of this without me? I'm not staying at the Bureau without you. I already put in the paperwork to retire."

I'm speechless, but not for long.

"But—what about Marcus? Don't you want to live near him? You two just barely made up."

"Just because we aren't estranged doesn't mean the man wants me living next door. Don't you want my help with your business?"

Yes. Yes, to all of it. I want to go into business with him. I want to live next door to each other. Slow it down, Evie.

"Jeremiah, there are things you don't know—"

"About Agent Bradley who wasn't Agent Bradley?"

"How the fuck—"

"You're not the only clever one on our team, kid. It was kind of obvious that something odd happened when the boss said that Agent Bradley wouldn't be able to wrap up the case for us because he was currently on an investigation, an investigation he's been on for the past month."

I figured Jeremiah had been on too many painkillers to understand that phone debriefing. I sit in silence, not really sure where to go with this conversation.

Jeremiah sighs. "I'm just glad he saved you. He was your 'Good Samaritan,' wasn't he?"

I slouch in my chair, not answering. Jeremiah laughs, enjoying my response. I don't have the heart to get annoyed at him for it. We're both breathing, both alive. We almost didn't get here.

"Anything else you want to cover before we go into business together?" *he asks once his laughter has subsided.*

I roll my lips before I sigh and tell him.

Silence. I look over and Jeremiah lets out a shocked whistle. I've finally surprised the man.

CHAPTER 16

Eugene

My walk is stiff as Jeremiah follows me. I don't want to give this man my back, but I hadn't planned for his presence. I actually hadn't planned much after seeing Evelyn again. It's difficult to make plans when you don't know how the other person in the situation is going to react. I gave it fifty-fifty odds she'd shoot me on sight.

I should have considered that she wouldn't move out to the middle of nowhere alone. I'm glad Gloria and Jeremiah are here for her, but either of them could prove a hindrance to convincing Evelyn that I'm here to be with her.

"Eugene."

I stop and slowly turn. We're now out of sight of the women. Is he going to kill me? I'm dangerous, a killer. I wouldn't blame him if he decided everyone would be better off without me hanging around.

Adrenaline has my hair standing on end, but Jeremiah doesn't make any sudden movements. Doesn't go for a gun. A bird sings in a nearby evergreen.

"You saved her," Jeremiah says.

I stay on guard but nod. "You called me."

The man gives me a considering look. "Thank you."

CHAPTER 16

"No thanks necessary."

Because there isn't. I'd save Evelyn every time. It's a truth written on my soul, traced when I'd first seen her at a press conference and carved deep with every new thing I learned about her. Whether it put my life at stake or not.

The depth of my feelings for Evelyn is something I don't understand. Maybe someday it will make sense, but for now, I'll do whatever is necessary to keep her alive. Happy. Which means standing in front of her partner like a man in front of a firing squad.

Jeremiah just nods. "Are you staying?"

"Yes."

The man's lips curve. "Even if Evie doesn't want you to?"

"I... I need to stay. Even if she says that there isn't anything here for me, I need to be near her."

Jeremiah waits and my cheeks heat. This man didn't gatekeep for Evelyn at work, but obviously he has no qualms about doing so when it involves her personal life.

"I-I have feelings for her." I don't realize I'm rubbing my chest until I say it out loud. My hand presses into where my heart aches for a woman I've barely spent any time with. Nothing about this makes sense.

Jeremiah sighs and shakes his head. "You're going to have to work on your words if you want to convince Evie of anything."

I freeze. "And that would be okay with you? Me trying to convince Evelyn of my feelings?"

Jeremiah's brow creases and his eyes take on a look as if he can see into the distance. "I took a chance, when I was shot. I took the chance that you could help Evie. That you would help Evie. You didn't disappoint. If you hadn't shown up, Evie would be dead."

Silence falls and the thought of what could have happened haunts the space between us.

Jeremiah continues, "I would have woken up from surgery with the knowledge that because I hadn't been paying attention, my partner died. When you saved Evie, you saved the last piece of my soul too. My son speaks to me, and now with Gloria… I have a chance to be alive again. All because you didn't disappoint." He looks down and kicks a rock. "The way I figure it is that you are worth betting on, and I can give you a chance to make Evie happy."

He looks up at me with a forbidding glare. "Just one chance though. You break her heart and I'll bury you. Vigilante or no."

I just stand there blinking. Why does it feel like he just gave me permission to date his daughter? *Let's focus on not having her pull a gun on you, Eugene, dating can come later.*

I clear my throat. "I appreciate that."

"You can move into my cabin with me in the meantime."

"What?" My voice goes up an octave.

"Wouldn't you rather be near Evie if she needs you?"

"Yes," I answer instantly.

"Good. It will give me a good opportunity to get to know your character."

I just agreed to move in with a retired federal agent.

I've lost my mind.

Evelyn

Gloria and I enter the kitchen and I help her start to put away the food. My anxiety builds. Gloria wants to talk about my confrontation. I bite my tongue to keep myself from being the one who brings it up.

"He seems nice. Respectful."

"Gloria—"

"And I can tell you like him."

Exasperation bleeds into my words. "I can't be with that man."

"Why not?"

"Other than the fact he's a criminal? It's not healthy! I shouldn't even like him."

"He did save your life."

"So, I should what? Fall into bed with him because I'm grateful?"

"No. I'm saying that you've always been attracted to him." Gloria gives me a steely-eyed look. I'll never tell a soul that her look is the one I perfected when talking to media.

I make a gesture in the air with my hands. "I have issues! Being attracted to a serial killer goes into that category."

"Yes, you have issues. You're working on your issues, but your issues have been compulsively searching out anonymous sex. Your issues haven't been wanting to be with a man who you've been playing mind games with for months and who saved your life." Gloria's voice vibrates with purpose. Her shoulders drop and I can tell her argument is going to move into tender areas of my heart. "Both things can be true, Evie. Your attraction to him, the chemistry you two feel, is real and you've had a history of risky sexual behavior. The feelings you have for him haven't abated since starting counseling, but your compulsive urges have."

"It's wrong, Gloria."

"Who says? Whose voice is in your head saying it's wrong to love the man who saved your life? A man who has sought you out. Why do you doubt yourself?"

That hits like a hammer. *Who indeed?* I don't really have to wonder. *Sinner, slut, daughter of Eve.*

"My judgment is suspect," I say hollowly.

Gloria continues as if I hadn't spoken, "From the way you explained it, you two have been circling each other for nearly a year. Now he's here—"

"Because you told him I'm pregnant. Why did you do that, Gloria?"

"Some men need a kick in the pants to act."

"A kick in the pants? Jesus, Gloria, I bet you gave the man a heart attack."

"What if he was as lost as you were? He broke his killing spree, didn't he? Maybe he needs more in his life than that. Maybe he needs to be here."

The idea is a precious one. One I want to keep and hold to myself. But it sounds like beautiful fiction.

"Malcom wouldn't have needed a kick in the pants to find me," I mumble.

Gloria scoffs. "Not to mar your hero-worship of the man, I loved Malcom, but to get him to propose I had to act like I was going on a date with someone else."

"What?" My voice raises in volume. *Why is this the thing I'm reacting to?*

Gloria sighs. "Malcom was an amazing man, but his tendency was always to wait and see when it came to making decisions. I just showed him what he wanted by making him think my affection for him was in danger."

"That is… devious. Wow."

And risky. This woman is always so direct and brave that it's almost uncomfortable to be around her sometimes.

CHAPTER 16

I ask the thing that plagues me.

"How do I know he's here for me?"

"What did he suggest?"

"That he stay until I believe him."

Gloria rolls her eyes. "Hm, so he's equipped to wait years?"

I snicker. "He doesn't seem to know me well."

"Yet. I'm sure you'll find a way to test the man."

That gives me pause. That sounds manipulative but I don't reject the idea instantly. I like the possibility of knowing for sure.

"Evie, take it from someone who lost one of the most important people in their lives. Don't turn him away without giving him a chance. Life is too short for regrets." Gloria doesn't list all the ways this could go poorly. Those are the things that keep me up at night.

"About you and Jeremiah…" I start.

"Oh, you noticed something past your moping?"

My lips twitch but my brow creases. "Are you sure you're ready to—"

"I've done my grieving, sweetheart. I make my own decisions about my life." Gloria's decisive voice is a warning that I heed.

Just then Jeremiah waltzes into the kitchen cheerfully. I glare at him.

"Done with the dismemberment so soon?"

"A messy business, but someone has to do it." Jeremiah gathers his grocery bags. "Tomorrow I'll bring over the steaks and we can make a night of it."

"Steaks sound lovely," Gloria pitches in. "Make sure to invite that nice young man."

I turn slowly on my heel toward Gloria. "You really want to push a serial killer at me?"

Gloria's face is full of innocence. "You'd rather I try to play matchmaker with the population of single men in town? You'd eat them alive."

I try not to smile at that and pick up a water glass.

"I'll bring him with me. He's moving into the spare room of my cabin for the time being."

I drop the glass.

CHAPTER 17

Eugene

There's a knock on the front door.

"Housekeeping!" Evelyn calls from the other side, and Jeremiah chuckles and gestures for me to open it.

I do, holding my breath when I see her again. It's only been a few hours since my aborted attempt at her door but feels longer. Maybe it's the awkwardness of moving in with my new roommate. My retired law enforcement roommate. Or maybe it's because I'm starving to see the woman.

Evelyn's face still packs a punch. She glares at me and the action makes the corner of my mouth kick up.

"I'm ignoring your presence," Evelyn says.

"Consider my presence ignored." I let her into Jeremiah's place.

Evelyn goes into the front room where Jeremiah sits in his recliner. Evelyn takes out items from the side table and starts proficiently checking off tasks. Medical things like blood pressure and temperature before getting to questions about his pain levels and areas.

I watch the interaction with curiosity. Jeremiah takes pity on me. "I'm an addict. Alcohol. Healing an injury while being an addict is a shitty experience. I'm sober when it comes to alcohol, but my medications have to be administered by my trusty partner."

"You could have had your medications administered by the pretty nurse up the street," she says.

Jeremiah scowls. "I didn't want her to think of me as her patient."

Evelyn sighs and I fill in the blanks. Gloria is a nurse.

"Maybe Gene can go make tea. Does tea sound good?" Evelyn asks Jeremiah. I jump that she isn't quite ignoring my existence. That she said my name. Crumbs of her attention sustain me.

Jeremiah deflates a little. "Well, that's your tell, kid."

"What?" Evelyn asks.

"You always make me tea when you're not going to give me a pill of the good stuff."

Evelyn looks up at the ceiling, considering. "Huh, you're right. Gloria always makes me tea when I have trouble sleeping. Has done that since I first moved in with her. I guess it's my go-to when I don't want you to stay up and think about the pain."

There's a silence and I don't leave to start the water boiling. I'm an avid audience to this dynamic. I've never seen Evelyn like this. Caretaking.

Jeremiah looks away. "I want it, Evie." His voice is raspy.

Evelyn's face softens. "I know."

Jeremiah clenches his fists before releasing them and sighing. "But I want something else more."

Evelyn scowls. "Jeremiah, Gloria can't be the reason for your recovery. You know that's kind of against the rules."

Jeremiah shrugs. "We have a lot of reasons for things throughout life. I get to pick mine. Go ahead and roll your eyes at me."

CHAPTER 17

I get to pick my reasons. Perhaps Jeremiah and I will get along after all.

"Stubborn mule," Evelyn says under her breath. "Would talking to your sponsor help?"

"Maybe in the morning. I'll touch base in the morning. I have another babysitter here anyway. I'm sure Eugene can talk about lots of things to keep me occupied."

My eyes widen in alarm. Evelyn tries not to smile but fails. Then she's back to frowning at Jeremiah.

"By the way, what happened to waiting to make your move with Gloria? You said you wanted to wait till later and now you've moved on to holding hands? It's scandalous."

Jeremiah blushes. "She said that she wasn't going to wait around for me to know what I want and that I'm not getting any younger."

Evelyn coughs. "Gloria's directness strikes again."

I can see where Evelyn gets that trait. I'm eager to get to know this Gloria.

"We're taking it slow," Jeremiah mumbles.

"I wouldn't bet on that," Evelyn says under her breath before turning to me. "You bring alcohol anywhere near here and I'll put a bullet in you."

I lift my brows, amused. "I thought you were ignoring my existence?"

Evelyn glares at me and for the first time, I think this might work out.

CHAPTER 18

Eugene

The cold pine-scented air grounds me and I finish off my coffee. The world is so quiet from this spot on the patio. Jeremiah has excellent taste in cabins. Or does Evelyn, who chose this location?

Evelyn.

We've been circling each other for a little more than a week. Or rather, I've been circling Evelyn, and she glares at me. Gloria's and Jeremiah's presence has been a boon. I can spend time around Evelyn without her snarling at me to leave because I'm always there at Gloria's invitation. God bless that woman.

A week, and I've made no headway. I walk on eggshells around Evelyn. So very careful not to lose my access to the one person that makes my heart beat. Instead, I spend time working and with Jeremiah, talking.

So much talking. We don't talk about Evelyn. Once or twice we've talked about business involving the Vigilante. We mostly talk about life in general. Politics, military, family histories, it's the oddest thing to talk so much about inane things after being secluded for so long.

I know Jeremiah is feeling out my character, and I don't blame the man. He does it for Evelyn, but I'd like

CHAPTER 18

to think we have something of a rapport now. To appease Jeremiah's need to look out for Evelyn, I hide nothing from him. Nothing.

Jeremiah suggested counseling and I laughed. I don't see what good it can do. I wasn't going to confess my crimes to a therapist. It was the one time he had brought Evelyn up to me.

It could help the rage. The feelings I know you're holding on to since your wife died. People don't start hunting down criminals for no reason Jeremiah had said during one of the fishing trips he dragged me on when I'd spent too long staring toward Evelyn's cabin.

You and Evelyn are making a business from hunting criminals. I avoided his penetrating gaze, the man has skills in that area, and looked out over the lazy river.

Which is how I know what I'm talking about. I didn't want to talk to a shrink either. Do you know who pushed me into it?

... *Evelyn.* I didn't even say it as a question. Of course it was Evelyn.

Exactly. You want a place in her life, you need to figure your own shit out.

I'll figure my own shit out. I just need to convince Evelyn to give me a chance.

The creak of floorboards has me turning.

"So, you decided to go with killing and dismembering me?" I'm only half-joking. Jeremiah looks at the ax in his hand.

"It's for you to use. Follow me."

I shrug. This past week has been full of helping Jeremiah with odd jobs for the cabin. He's mobile enough, but there are many tasks to do before it starts to snow that would press Jeremiah's recovery and pain levels into uncomfortable areas.

It feels good to have something to do with my hands while being in limbo with my mind and heart.

The leaves crackle under our feet as we walk to the chopping block. A stack of logs is already there.

I scowl. "I could have moved those."

Jeremiah shakes his head. "I had them delivered. Thanks for caring, Mom."

"Don't let it go to your head. It's purely self-preservation. What do you think Evelyn would do to me if I let you hurt yourself?"

Jeremiah chuffs but the humor falls from his face as he faces me.

This feels significant. I take hold of the ax and the wood grain mimics the knot of concern in my chest.

"I'm going to tell you something because I don't believe in setting people up to fail. If Evie had her way, she'd throw the information in your face to see how you'd react. To analyze it. I'm trying to give you a little space from that. Give you the opportunity to react better."

The words ring ominously. I've known Evelyn has been wanting to test me. To give herself some metric she can point to in order to reject me from her life.

Jeremiah continues, "How you choose to react to this information is crucial. This is your moment of truth. Your choice."

Is this about the maybe pregnancy? I can't read Jeremiah's weathered face.

I take a deep breath. "Then I guess you should get it over with."

Jeremiah sets a log in position before giving me a long stare.

CHAPTER 18

"The man you released the info packet about, Alec Montgomery, was released and charges have been dropped."

My brain stalls out at that.

Distantly, I'm aware of Jeremiah's exit. I grip the ax and pace. The numbness from the shock of it all bleeding away.

I tried this time. I tried to go about justice the right way. To leave the world to deal with this. Now a guilty man has gone free and I'm supposed to just let it slide?

I could leave and just take care of it. All the details of that man's life are still in my mind. It would be so easy. That man would finally pay for what he's done. Anger starts to burn. I turn and take two steps toward my Jeep. The weight of the ax in my hand brings me to the present. I stop.

If I leave, if I go back to being the Vigilante, I don't get to have Evelyn and whatever future we could have together. She'll know. This is the choice Jeremiah was talking about.

Frustration charges my pacing as I turn back to the wood chopping block. There's an itch. A need riding just under my skin and I want to scratch it until it bleeds but *the price*. The price is too great.

I shout as I bring the ax down on the log and the loud crack echoes through the woods. The sound brings a moment of calm. It helps with this need to return to my mission. I pick up the larger wood split and split it again. I continue the process, picking up a fresh log to piece apart.

Soon my arms and chest burn from the exertion. The cold air sears my lungs, but it helps cool the rage. Sweat has my T-shirt sticking to me. I hear the rustle and crunch of leaves and stop. She's here. I know she's here. She wants to analyze my reaction.

"I guess you know." Evelyn's voice caresses me, but I don't turn around.

"I know."

"You're still here." Her voice is soft, but it hardens something in me.

I turn. The sight of her is a lethal strike. My body is already on fire but I find in the presence of my angel that it was barely banked coals before. The white sweater she wears appears so soft I just want to rub my face against it before pulling it off and sucking her tits.

Calm, Eugene. Careful, Eugene.

"Isn't this what you wanted? You wanted me to be tested? Well, *here* I am." I'm not so calm.

"This time."

The frustration is back in force. "I choose you! I'm here for you!"

"Then why do you sound so angry about that?" Evelyn keeps her voice calm, but I can tell the currents under her surface are turning.

Suddenly something clears in my head. "Is this what it's going to be like then? Are you just going to wait for me to screw up? Waiting for the one time I slip?"

"Yes."

The years stretch out before me. Always being pushed away for my prior crimes. The expectation always there that I'll leave.

"That's bullshit. You're just using that as an excuse not to make a decision about *us*," I accuse.

"You're always going to be pulled toward being a vigilante," Evelyn decrees it like she would say that the sky is blue.

"You know this for a fact?" I ask.

My logical avenging angel looking to rip my heart out.

"From what I know about you, that's what I project."

My voice drops low. "You don't know me very well."

"Don't I?" She looks angry now. Good. Evelyn takes a step closer before throwing her hands up. "Fine. Tell me a story, Gene."

"A story?"

"Tell me your creation story. What mythos is responsible for the creation of the Vigilante?"

I hesitate in the face of her glower. The idea of recounting the events that took slices out of my soul in front of Evelyn is painful.

More so, I know this won't advance my objectives. But this is the first thing Evelyn has asked of me since I got here, other than telling me to leave.

Evelyn

Gene's face shuts down. His chest still expanding with his deep breaths. My fingers itch to touch him, but I'm not letting hormones make decisions today.

Gene's shoulders drop and he looks away before he starts. "My wife was murdered while I was deployed."

Wife. My mouth dries up as I try to process this.

"You married young." I'm buying myself time to process why the fact that Gene having had a wife causes a ball of pain to embed in my chest.

"She was pregnant." Gene stares at me now, and I try not to visibly react.

The pain spreads. For a moment, when I'd seen that he was still here, I'd been hopeful that his presence here had really meant that he chose me.

Now I know. I know that Gloria implying to Gene that I'm pregnant triggered him coming here. I thought he could either have been here because he wanted to be with me or just because he thought I was pregnant, but I didn't consider a third option. That I could just be a symbol for the wife he failed before.

That option is the worst, but it being the worst usually means it's the most likely answer. My eyes sting. Why am I still here? I have confirmation enough that this will never work.

My mouth makes words. Trying to find connections in Gene's history. "And what about the crime Jacob Trier mentioned?"

The Copycat who had wanted to hang me.

"My wife wasn't just murdered. They… I—" Gene breaks off. "Afterward, I went back on deployment. A soldier had been talking about how well the local women screamed and I… snapped."

My pain isn't just for me now. Gene avoids my eyes. It's all so terrible. So ugly. Empathy threatens to suck me in, but I stay cool.

"And when you started killing in the states?" I ask.

Gene shrugs. "Everywhere I turned there was injustice. Places the system didn't reach. I needed to do something."

There it is. His creed. His mission. The real reason this will never work.

"And you think that's fixed now?" I prod.

Gene glares at me. "I think that I've made my decision on the matter clear."

His previous words echo in my mind, *I choose you! I'm here for you!*

Yeah, he thinks he's made a decision about it.

"Serial killers don't just stop, Gene. You really think that you'll be able to resist the urge to take action? You've fed the compulsion before, again and again."

"You believe that I'll always re-offend? That I'm just another statistic?" Gene looks intensely at me.

"I don't believe that you'll be satisfied with a quiet life in a mountain cabin with the compulsions you're going to struggle with." And that destroys me a little on the inside.

"Don't I have any say in the matter? Aren't I more than just a black and white equation?"

I've made him angry. I push forward. Unlike the moment in the motel room, I know this man now. Gene won't hurt me.

"Psychology says—"

"The same psychobabble that failed you in catching me?"

The pain in my chest snaps and anger spills out.

"Oh, fuck you!" I snarl.

Gene takes two steps and he's in my space. Heaving chest, the sweaty man looks like he wants to eat me alive and I want to let him.

"Any time, any place, any way you want, Evelyn. Just say the word. A life with you is what *I choose*."

My face heats and whatever words I was going to say catch in my throat. Lust brews but can't go anywhere. I'm not done.

"Do you know why they let Alec Montgomery go?" I ask.

"Because the system is broken." He spits the bitter words out.

Gene's truth. The longer he stays with me, the more he's going to see the situation as him sacrificing the mission he took up. Not that there are flaws in his design.

"No. Because he didn't do it. His brother confessed. Authorities are keeping it quiet while they navigate the media shit storm you started when you demonized the wrong man."

Shock paints Gene's features.

"But all the evidence. The mistress? The wire transfer? The convenient alibi?"

"All fallible, correlative evidence you put together to support what you wanted to find. You would have killed an innocent man."

Gene's face twists. "He's not an innocent."

"Innocent of the crime you accused him of. What would you have done if you had killed the man? Would you have looked at his life, tried to find some reason to excuse your actions?"

"Sins—"

"We're all sinners!" I shout. I'm so sick of everything being infected with the moral codes drilled into me as a child. I chose law in place of religion. Logic over belief.

I continue, "Did you even notice that your methods were getting less careful? That the info packets you've been releasing have been getting smaller and smaller? That the evidence you required for you to act as judge and jury was becoming less substantial?"

Gene shakes his head. Denial carves his brow. I'm breaking his worldview. Smashing foundational blocks as if they're chalk. It's fair. He's already broken mine.

"Tell me now that you won't struggle with compulsions. That you weren't getting less careful because it became less and less about justice and more about the rush. Tell me that you're positive you can be satisfied with a life with me." Tears track down my face now and I wipe them away angrily.

CHAPTER 18

Gene doesn't even notice my tears, and that shatters me a little more. He's too busy wrestling with the revelations I've dug up and cast upon him like a toxic hex.

The leaves crunch underfoot as I turn and do the hard but necessary thing.

I leave him there to struggle with his demons and flounder. I can try and try to keep him afloat, but there are things that people need to decide for themselves.

CHAPTER 19

Eugene

Patience is a virtue. Every hunter knows it. I've always had the ability for patience, but my limit is approaching. My skin actively crawls as I rock on one of the rocking chairs Jeremiah set out on his porch. My laptop is closed on my lap and I stare out into the trees.

I pretend I can see through the trees, see the cabin where Evelyn and Gloria live. It's a meditative practice. I rock and think. Without a better plan, all I can do is wait.

Well, there's more I can do and I'm doing it.

Yesterday Evelyn said I'd always be pulled toward being a vigilante. She flayed me to the bone with her accusations that the rush had started being a driving force in my actions. She's right.

Evelyn showed me the truth of the matter and left me in the pit I'd dug for myself. It was painful. Is painful. But I understand now that this is something I'm going to struggle with.

I was on a path that was heading toward being splintered apart with my own convictions. That Evelyn was there to pass judgment is the thing that pulled me away from the edge. That made me realize there are other directions open to me.

CHAPTER 19

So here I am after video conferencing with a therapist, staring out into the trees. I now have a weekly appointment with a man who has an extensive history of counseling veterans. The truth is that I never really returned to civilian life. I brought the war zone, the feelings of violence and need to act, home with me.

Dr. Wallace told me it's a common phenomenon after I confessed to the compulsions I feel. So many possible vigilantes out there, and I was just one that escalated into action.

Jeremiah comes out on the porch and sits back in another rocker, the wood creaks in a familiar way that sounds comforting now. "So?"

I purse my lips. "It could be helpful."

Jeremiah nods at that. "And?"

"I have a standing appointment. Weekly. Dr. Wallace says we can keep the appointments as video calls."

I appreciate that Jeremiah doesn't tell me that he told me so after I'd ridiculed the option before. His support makes this easier. Knowing that Evelyn cared about me enough to force the bright truth into my face also helps.

A rustle has us both looking up. Gloria comes into view, and I hold my breath, waiting for Evelyn to follow. I breathe out in disappointment when she doesn't.

"Hello, beautiful," Jeremiah says.

"Hi, you," Gloria responds fondly.

If Gloria is here, then Evelyn is home alone. There's a strong urge to head over there. We have things to discuss.

"Evening, Gloria, I didn't know you two had plans tonight," I say.

"Oh, we didn't, but I figured I'd stop by and maybe make some. Evie went into town. I think she wanted to decompress at the bar."

White noise. Gloria and Jeremiah are talking about their plans for the night, but all that fills my ears is white noise. *Decompress.* I've seen how Evelyn decompresses in a bar.

"I've got to go."

Evelyn

I broke him. I broke him on purpose and he's still here. I expected that Gene would have left. Continued being the Vigilante. But the text I got from Jeremiah telling me my criminal hasn't left means I need to reevaluate. He stayed.

It could be for any of the reasons going through my mind, but it could also be that he wants to be with me. That no matter the revelations he's dealing with, that choice he made still holds true.

I need to know for sure though. I want to believe it. I'm just scared to.

I woke up this morning with the knowledge that something has to happen.

Gene is everywhere I turn. Hanging out with Jeremiah, coming to BBQs, playing cards with Gloria. The only part of my life the man has yet to invade is the fledgling business Jeremiah and I are building.

The awful thing is that I want him to. I'm starting to like Eugene Peterson for more than just what he is capable of doing to my body. I'm slowly starting to trust Gene. That he's still here helps that trust.

Jeremiah has even given his approval of him.

CHAPTER 19

The man still hasn't asked. Yesterday we'd flung words back and forth and he still hadn't asked about *that*. Gene must have some assumption about the whole business. Whatever he's assuming, I need to confront this. I need to know, the best I can, what the man is here for.

So here I am. Standing at the bar, hand around a drink, waiting. There is not a single doubt in my mind that he'll come. *And if he doesn't?* The inaction will be as telling as action.

I draw patterns in the condensation on the glass and take in the bar patrons. A lot of the men have noticed me. It's a small town and they've seen me around. There is a sense of anticipation in the air. I don't know if they're holding their breath waiting for someone to meet me here for a date or getting up the courage to approach. I don't care either way.

The exact moment Gene enters is clear. The air crackles and the men in the bar surreptitiously look away to avoid the predator in the room.

I anticipated that Gene would come up beside me, facing me. Confront me where I could see him. Instead, he steps behind me, his body mirroring my angled position to the bar. One of Gene's hands falls to my waist, the other slides to my wrist of the hand that had been tracing the rim of the glass holding my drink on the bar. The position is terribly intimate. Sensual.

"We need to talk." Gene's voice has dropped into the gravelly range and his words reverberate with something. Anger? I don't have enough information without turning to face him, but I'm enjoying feeling the heat of his body behind mine.

"I haven't finished my drink."

Gene stiffens when I gesture to my half-gone drink before his body relaxes some and he sighs. Is he disappointed or relieved that he thinks I'm not pregnant? I have a strong urge to turn to take in his facial expression, but the craving of my body to stay in the cradle of his arms is too strong. I've already missed the crucial moment with my bad positioning. I might as well enjoy the contact while I have it.

"And I came here for something," I say. I don't know if I lean my body back into his on purpose but the feel of his strong chest against my back is practically erotic.

The hand Gene has on my waist squeezes, possessive, as his hot breath bathes my neck and ear.

"Evelyn, please don't push me right now. We need to talk, and I'd rather do it in private."

He's been so damn careful. Like a bird of prey, handling me with feathers instead of talons, but feathers are an ineffective way to hold on to what you want. I want to feel the talons. I want to see his teeth, the vicious parts of himself that I saw during our single night together.

I push. "What about what I came here looking for?"

"I'll give you more than what you came here looking for," he says darkly. He presses back against me and his hot erection adds a layer to the angry frustration he speaks with.

I keep my smile small. "Okay."

The bartender makes eye contact with me, and I nod. I already paid for the drink. Gene moves from me and grabs my hand as we move for the exit. Another act of possession. Just being around Gene makes it hard to think, but I can't help taunting.

"What, you don't want to use the storeroom for old time's sake?"

"I'll need more privacy. Keep teasing me, Evelyn, I bet I can still find your handcuffs."

I stumble and flash hot at that. "I thought you said you wanted to talk?"

"When we get to your place." Gene pulls me to the Jeep he had bought. I let him. I'll retrieve my car from here later. Gene opens the passenger door for me, and I get in. The drive is a quiet one. We don't live far from town.

I'm having a hard time interpreting Gene's emotional state. The man's face gives nothing away, but his intense dark eyes glitter. What had been the point of all this again? Oh yes, finding out how Gene feels about me. Why he tracked me down.

"You stayed," I say. With those simple words, my worries about the whole Vigilante business unravel because Gene smiles.

"I stayed."

"No more Vigilante?"

"No more Vigilante. I'm getting help. You're right. I was devolving as a killer."

It's such a simple response but it doesn't make it less impactful.

We pull up to my house and Gene turns off the engine. His jaw clenches and his knuckles are white on the steering wheel. "Invite me in, Evelyn."

"Are you a vampire?"

The glance Gene shoots me vibrates with annoyance. "No, I'm a man who wants to know you're inviting me in for a conversation and I'm not being pushy."

"Maybe I want you pushy."

"Fuck, Evelyn, you're killing me. I want us to have a conversation before anything else happens."

"What kind of conversation?"

Gene struggles with that for a moment before answering with a shrug. "I want to be with you. Exclusively."

"You want to date?"

"To start."

My brows lift. He's putting it all out there.

"Well then, I guess we should talk in the house."

Gene is out of the vehicle and opening my door before I finish. *He wants to date*. I'm still catching up to the idea.

First, I assumed that Gene would leave to continue being the Vigilante. Second, I thought he'd stop pursuing me as soon as he thought I wasn't pregnant. Wrong on all accounts. It's annoying that my bias is ruining my track record.

I now face the predicament that Gloria pointed out. I have to trust that the feelings I have for Gene are honest. I have to trust myself.

We make it to the kitchen before I can think of how to respond. "What does us dating look like?"

Exasperation lines Gene's face. "You seem like you're deliberately underplaying my feelings, so I'm going to be specific."

I'm ready to catalog whatever Gene is going to say but he closes in on me. The counter presses against my back as he invades my space. The closeness is distracting. The feel of his breath on my face and the waves of *something* coming from him.

"I want your everything, Evelyn. Everything you're willing to give me and everything you secretly want me to take from you." Gene's voice growls and my face heats. His hand slides up and rests across my collarbones, applying light pressure around my throat just like he'd done when we'd been in bed together. My inhale stutters but Gene keeps talking.

"All your compulsions, secrets, flaws, and soul. I want to be your everything..." Gene stops, struggling with whatever other bomb he's going to drop. I'm already blinking, stunned and my breath shaky, before he continues. My chest aches at the broken way his voice flows.

"But I don't know how. I don't know if a man like me, who has done what I've done, is capable of love. All I know is I dream of you. Waking, sleeping, it doesn't matter. You are my obsession. You consume me."

The ache in me moves lower as Gene's body brushes mine.

"Gene," I whisper.

Gene's other hand starts to unbutton my shirt as he devastates me with words I never expected. *How does this man keep surprising me?*

"Thinking you were pregnant just pushed me from the limbo I had been in long enough to see where my true obsession lay. That's why I closed up shop. Not because of the idea of a baby, but because it made me realize that the possibility of having you is better than any meandering journey or vigilante act."

The tug of the shirt buttons is a distant thing. Gene's eyes take in the skin he exposes. I hadn't bothered with a bra under the thick flannel, the chill of the air on my bare skin battles with the heat of his breath. I watch his face as he looks down at me, and his expression does more to seduce me than all the physical touches could do combined. A mixture of awe and heat that draws me in and melts my reservations.

Gene stops unbuttoning just under my breasts and spreads his hot hand on my chest, right over my heart. He can undoubtedly feel my heart race. We still in the sacred intimacy for one moment, then two. I've never felt so naked with another person. Then Gene tugs on the saint medallion I can't throw away and starts to speak again.

"When I saw you kept my gift, I knew there was a chance. For me. For us. That you would keep something like this on your person even with the risks... it's telling."

"I short-circuited the tracker. Give me a little credit," I mumble, not disagreeing with his assessment.

"When?"

Ah, answering that would be telling. I'd kept the tracker intact for an embarrassingly long time. I wanted for him to be able to find me. There are so many reasons for me to hate this man, to never want to see him again, but I don't hate him. Instead I left that avenue open, let the possibility stay alive until the moment everything changed.

Until I peed on a goddamn stick.

"I don't want to say." It comes out breathy. I don't want to lie, but I don't want to tell him yet either.

"Keeping secrets, angel?" Gene's mouth curves, his tone is teasing. There's still a darkness to him. A permanent shadow that makes up his existence, but the man in front of me is more than just his demons. "You can keep your secrets, for now. Later, I'll put those handcuffs you liked so much to use and get the answers I want. Would you like that?"

I force myself to be brave. So many unknowns make up the puzzle of our lives but there are things I need to confess to. "Yes," I whisper.

Gene closes the distance between our mouths and suddenly I can taste him. The slide of tongues and tease

CHAPTER 19

of bodies. Gene keeps the kiss measured with his hand collaring my throat even as I want to rush. My hands grip his waistband, trying to pull him closer but he controls this.

I want to feel his skin against me. I want to feel him inside of me again. I want him to dismantle every defense mechanism I have so I can let every sense bathe in the potency of this. I want him to keep me safe.

Gene pulls away and I produce a disappointed sound. The hand on my throat tightens just slightly.

"You mind fucked me."

I rear back at that. Gene sounds shocked and gives a little laugh. "You haven't been drinking alcohol, I would have tasted it."

Oh, well… this wasn't the direction I wanted to go. I roll my lips.

"Fuck, that's hot." His voice is rough and dark, he kisses me hard and our bodies grind together.

I pull back when I come up for breath. "You like me manipulating you?"

"Your mind is part of the reason I'm so obsessed with you," he says as he moves the hand collaring me to trace the edge of my lips.

"Gloria says we've been doing mental foreplay the whole time I chased you."

"And?" he asks.

"She's right."

A growl sounds from Gene's throat and his hand moves to my hair and grips it. The pull has a sigh falling from my lips.

"Tell me you don't want me, Evelyn. Tell me to leave. Tell me I can't keep you."

"Why would I do that?"

"Because otherwise I'm going to keep you any way I can. You won't wake up a day without me inside your body."

Dirty things, the words make my knees weak.

My next words are barely audible. "Sounds like you have this all planned out."

Gene boosts me onto the counter. "Just the important things." He continues unbuttoning my shirt. "You haven't said no, Evelyn."

"I'm not going to—" I end on a moan as Gene pulls my shirt down one shoulder and sucks my nipple into his mouth. I gasp when he draws hard on it while using the grip on my hair to arch my back. Gene moans into my skin before letting go with a pop.

"Are you really going to continue keeping your secret, Evelyn?"

I'm blushing now, there's no mystery what he's talking about. Our time together had been short, I didn't expect him to notice any physical changes like the increased curve of my breast yet, but I had underestimated his memory of my body.

"N-Not yet."

Gene's smile is wicked as he gives my nipple the lightest bite that makes my body jolt. "I could get it out of you. Torment you until you tell me."

"Jesus Christ, Gene, please. We can talk about it later. I just need to feel you. I-I dream about it. Please, Gene."

Gene lets go of my hair and pulls back. His cheekbones have flags of red. I claw at him, but he catches my wrists in a hand. "Fuck, hearing you beg is too much. I'll make you beg again another time. I'll take it slow then."

"Gene—"

He snaps then and my jeans are pulled from me roughly, my underwear going with them; no finesse in the abrasive tugs. I'd wince if I wasn't so desperate. Gene lets my wrists go and my hands are unbuckling his pants, uncoordinated, trying to release him.

The cold counter against my ass should slow me down but it just feeds the need to join my body with his.

The first thrust has my head falling back. I'm so wet, but the force of the stretch has me wincing. Gene stills, deep inside me he throbs and I pant. He has a hand in my hair again, keeping me positioned how he wants.

"God, Evelyn, you feel so perfect. You take me so well." A small pump of his hips and his cock slides in farther. I gasp.

Gene kisses my lips, soft, as my body gives to his. "Where do you want me to come, angel?"

I open my eyes. His gleam playful. Of course he knows. He knows I'd stop this if we needed a condom. The feel of his bare cock inside me is too good to deal with anything as useless right now as condoms.

I crease my brow. "Fuck."

Gene laughs tightly. "I told you I wanted all of your secrets. I'll take them if I have to—" He breaks off on a groan as I flex around him.

I sigh, so put upon. If I'm going to let him win this game, I'm going to make it good. "I want to feel you come inside me. I want it all. I want so much it drips out of me for days. I want to feel marked by you."

Gene is no longer as jovial. His hips drive forward at my words. "*Fuck*," he snarls.

"Give it to me," I egg him on.

The tension in the air snaps. I cry out at the force of Gene's thrust into me. The cry turns to whispered begs as his body fucks into mine. I pant and gasp, my body wrapping around his as his cock stretches me in the best of ways.

"I'm going to keep you, angel. I'm going to stay and remind you every day that I'm here for good. I'm going to remind you every moment you give me that you're my avenging angel. That this hot cunt is mine."

Filthy and perfect words wind my body up like a taut string waiting to be plucked until Gene drops a hand and uses his thumb to circle my clit. I claw at his shoulders and neck as he winds me tighter until I snap with a shout. The climax is intense and pulses in time to Gene's rocking.

"That's it, angel. I'd carve my heart out to see you come and you think I won't want to stay?"

"Stop talking," I gasp but I don't mean it. Gene's chuckle and hard cock tells me he knows I don't mean it. He slides from me and I make a pitiful sound, but he pulls me toward him before turning me over the counter. *Oh.*

Gene slides his cock into me again. So slow that we both groan at this new angle.

"God, Evelyn, if you could see this you wouldn't wonder if I'd stay." Gene's tone is worshiping.

"So you'll stay just for my pussy?"

I yelp when he smacks my ass.

"Your cunt, your mind, your heart. I'm. Here. For. You." He punctuates each word with a thrust and his fingers dig into my hips. I'm so full, my body climbs again, and I give into the sensation. Trust this moment as Gene starts to power into me until I'm coming as he stiffens and fills me how I asked him to.

I roll my head on the counter and pant. Gene's breathing is just as choppy, but suddenly he pulls me up and I'm being carried. I squeal, scared of being dropped I hug myself to his neck. The man has the gall to huff at me.

CHAPTER 19

"Where's your bedroom?"

"Down the hall to the right. We should clean up the kitchen first." I blink, my eyelids suddenly heavy.

"I think Gloria is going to be gone for a while yet. The two of you planned this, didn't you?"

I hide my face in his neck. It's damp but smells like him and the pine from outside. "Hmm?"

"Oh, don't play innocent. You've manipulated this from the beginning."

Gene drops me on my bedspread. I scowl at him as the post-orgasm haze leaves me. Gene is still smiling, but it's more of a crook of his lips before he turns and goes into the en-suite bathroom before coming out with a washcloth. It's déjà vu from our first time together.

This time I just narrow my eyes at Gene instead of arguing. He holds himself over me on the bed, urging me to lie back, kissing me softly. The coldness of the cloth against my pussy has me gasping, and Gene laughs. *Asshole.*

"Admit it, Evelyn."

I sigh, "Yes, we planned it."

Gene goes back to the bathroom with the washcloth. "When is Gloria coming back?"

"Tomorrow morning."

Gene's brows lift and he starts to disrobe.

"What are you doing?"

He scoffs, "What does it look like?"

I get distracted with his body. I've never seen all of him in the light of day. I crave to drag my teeth down the lines of his muscles. I can tell he's lost weight. The muscles of his body are more unforgiving than they had been the last time we were together.

"Evelyn."

I snap my gaze away from his body to see his mocking face. He's enjoying my distraction too much. I flush and throw a pillow at him. He catches the projectile before climbing under the blankets and dragging me with him. My shirt is removed and we're skin-to-skin in a bed again.

"It looks like you're getting comfy."

Gene's face reddens. "I'd like to hold you, like this, is that okay? It's been a while since I've been able to."

I nod and we spoon together again. It's so nice that I have to keep from taking a nap. When Gene speaks, I jump and realize what he wants. Pillow talk.

"You lied to me."

I snort. "You made assumptions."

"You deliberately misled me."

Oh, he wants to talk about misleading.

"You pretended to be a federal agent and seduced me. I hardly think ordering a mocktail is of the same magnitude."

Gene scoffs. "You knew."

"You didn't know I knew. And I didn't know for sure. Just suspected."

Gene kisses my shoulder. "So?"

So. I take a deep breath and sigh it out. I don't know what to say.

"It's different than I expected it to be. I thought…" I trail off.

"You thought you'd be doing this with someone you were already in a partnership with." Gene fills in for me. I nod.

"Are you… happy about it?" Gene asks.

I deliberate and turn toward him. "Yes, and terrified."

Gene's eyes are soft. "You, my angel, are one of the bravest people I've ever known."

CHAPTER 19

I swallow. "Are you... happy about it?"

Gene has an inscrutable look on his face. "Are you going to let me be a part of it? I'm trying to get my shit together. I'm trying to be... enough."

I let out the breath I'm holding. It didn't occur to me that he thought I'd hold him apart from it all. It should have. If he had left, I would have. But he's here, and I can't imagine not doing this together.

"Yes... I don't know if I'm enough."

I voice the fear that whispers over and over again in my mind. Gene's arms squeeze around me.

"You, former Special Agent Evelyn Michaels, will always be enough. And yes, I'm very happy about it. It's unexpected, but so is all of this. You and me together."

I nod. "It's unexpected but we feel... right."

We fall silent and it's an easy silence. It feels calm. Until Gene breaks the silence.

"We should, perhaps, lie to them about how we met."

EPILOGUE

Marcus

"Gloria wants me to ask you if you're coming for Christmas?" Dad's voice sounds hesitant, hesitant but edged in hope.

I waver. I haven't spent the holidays with family since Mom died.

Dad swallows. "You don't have to. You and I getting along is still so new… And everyone at your precinct will be asking for work off for the holidays… I'll just tell Gloria that maybe next year you'll come."

I find my voice, keeping it low because I'm somewhere I'm not supposed to be. "I'd like to come and see you guys for Christmas. If that's okay, I mean. Or at least near the time if work is too busy on the holidays."

The sound of Dad clearing his throat makes mine swell.

"I think she'd really like that."

I almost laugh at the obfuscation. Luckily, I'm well versed in how much Dad cares about me. Now.

"Well, I'll let you go. No doubt Gloria will want you to get some sleep."

"No doubt. I love you, Marcus. Stay safe. Make good choices."

I laugh softly. "I love you too, Dad."

Small miracle that we can say the words "I love you" now after all the bad feelings we've had fester in the past.

We both hang up. My laugh has a bitter tang that I hope wasn't audible to Dad. *Make good choices.*

I wouldn't say that making good choices is my current forte. I look into the bright window. I'm sure that I'm deep enough in the shadows to remain unseen.

Dad sounds good. I'm glad he has Gloria and Evie. We all had an opportunity to get to know each other in the hospital. Surprisingly, Evie and I got along once both of our tempers cooled and I redirected my regrets and guilt into a better pursuit than being an ass.

The only person that will be at whatever holiday event I attend that I haven't met yet will be Evie's boyfriend, Eugene something-or-another. The careful way that Dad mentions the man sparks my curiosity, but I have enough on my mind than being foolish enough to do a background check on him. Evie is sharp. If she didn't want to be with the man, she wouldn't.

Evie isn't the one I'm compelled to protect.

That individual saunters in front of the curtainless window in some white lacy thing that has me gritting my teeth in discomfort. The robe she wears over the lingerie is gauzy and does nothing to block my view, or the view that anyone would have if they looked through her townhouse window.

Cassidy Kade. Tormentor of my conscience. Last known victim of the serial killer that had been dubbed the "Widower." The victim that had survived.

She looks different now than when I pulled her from the tomb the killer had bricked her into six months ago. Her circulated missing photo had shown a young-looking woman with hair between brown and blonde, primly pulled in a twist. The smile captured by the camera had been with a closed mouth. Everything about her personality had been buttoned up and wrapped in a cardigan.

The current Cassidy Kade holds only a tiny resemblance to that photo and is light years away from the traumatized figure I'd pulled from the edge of death.

The woman curling up on her couch holds herself as if she's a different person. Her hair cascades in dark waves. It looks as if she's dyed it a shade of red this month. The fashion she's chosen tonight looks vintage-inspired, bold red lipstick and winged eyeliner included with the corset looking undergarment that holds her breasts up high and cinches her waist. Glamorous, ghostly temptation.

She looks bold. All fire and spark.

I'm glad. Seeing her this way satisfies a part of me that always worries about this woman. Always thinks about her. I won't lie to myself and say the only emotions I feel toward her are protective. I'm not delusional enough for that.

I should leave. This is wrong. I've been checking in on Cassidy—Ms. Kade, I correct—routinely since the horrible incident.

Since she'd wrapped her arms around my neck, covered in cement dust, sobbing, and shaking. That moment had jolted something inside me. Shattered inhibitions that should have stayed whole.

My obsession, because I'm still in a right enough mind to know that is what this is, progressed over time. It started with the urge to look in on her every once in a while—once every couple of weeks after the incident. Then once a week. Now, I perform this ritual multiple times a week.

I never let her know I'm checking up on her. I don't want to remind her of the worst day of her life.

It breaks up my personal time from my other obsession. Finding the Widower. Because of me, we didn't catch him. I chose to take the slim chance and save Ms. Kane on that fateful day instead of approaching with caution and apprehending the Widower.

The Widower hasn't struck since he failed with Ms. Kane. In my nightmares, he gets her again and I'm not fast enough to save her.

Ms. Kane slides a hand gracefully through her hair and drops it to where her breasts swell over the lacy thing she wears. I watch, mesmerized, hating my weakness.

She looks right at me, and I stop breathing. She can't see me where I am, I know she can't see me, but it's as if her green eyes drive a nail through my soul.

My phone begins to vibrate, and I force myself to turn from the woman's gaze and walk away. My body is tight and my heart races as I walk. My phone displays my partner's name.

"This is White." My response is automatic, even though I know the caller.

"Hey Marcus, I wanted to call you. To tell you before you heard it from someone else… I know you've been looking into the Widower case in your free time…" Toby Martin's voice trails off and has an air of disapproval. My "hobby" has been one of the few points of contention between us.

I pull my hand down my face. "Spit it out, Toby."

A sigh comes through the speaker. "A woman's body was found at the edge of a river, an hour south of here. It looks like it's him."

"What?" My heart sinks into the shadows around me. My breath is trapped in my chest.

"They're saying the Widower is back."

The End

Don't miss Marcus's and Cassidy's book!
Signup for my newsletter to get bonus content and updates about my writing.
lillianlark.com/newsletter

Note from the Author

Hello Dear Reader!

Thank you for reading Her Vigilante! This book came to fruition in a roundabout way.

The premise of this story was the first bit of romance writing I ever did. Before Tangled Wires or Three of Hearts, there was this story about a killer and the FBI agent hunting him. I sent this sexy short story to my friend Kelsy, and she wanted a longer version.

It was that vote of confidence that made the idea of writing a whole book possible. I started Tangled Wires and began this wonderful journey.

Two books later, and this story premise kept whispering seductively in my ear. So here we are!

A special thank you to Kelsy Rice, who helped kickstart everything.

Thank you, Dear Reader, for your support! Please leave a review if you enjoyed (or if you didn't) to help other readers in their quest to find books that work for them.

L. Lark

About the Author

Lillian Lark was born and raised in the saltiest of cities in Utah. Lillian is an avid reader, cat mom to three demons, and loves writing sexy stories that twist you up inside.

Printed in Great Britain
by Amazon